"Connor, we can death wish."

He jerked his chin toward the people they'd left behind. "They're your team."

"And I'm yours." Sabrina tightened her grip, looked right at him. "I don't know what the hell I'm going to do about it. But I am sticking. You hear me?"

"Yeah, I hear you. Hard not to when you're yelling in my ear." And Connor heard something in her words that she wasn't saying. So, he figured he'd be the bigger man and say them first.

He cupped her face with his hands. "I care about you, Sabrina."

She jerked a little in his grasp, like he'd punched her rather than said something nice and meaningful.

"I guess I care about you too," she muttered. Then she pulled herself away, shoving at his arms. "So, we go together. Stop arguing and let's get this over with."

"Then what?"

"Let's live through this first."

Connor planned on it...

MOUNTAINSIDE MURDER

Nicole Helm

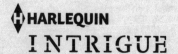

HARLEQUIN
INTRIGUE

To the kid who lives behind me who is always, always dribbling
his basketball, for reminding me what it means to have
dedication to something you love even if the thud, thud,
thud while I'm trying to write drives me to distraction.
Keep thudding, buddy.

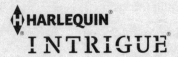

Recycling programs
for this product may
not exist in your area.

ISBN-13: 978-1-335-48928-9

Mountainside Murder

Copyright © 2021 by Nicole Helm

This edition published by arrangement with Harlequin Books S.A.

For questions and comments about the quality of this book,
please contact us at CustomerService@Harlequin.com.

Harlequin Enterprises ULC
22 Adelaide St. West, 40th Floor
Toronto, Ontario M5H 4E3, Canada
www.Harlequin.com

Printed in U.S.A.

Nicole Helm grew up with her nose in a book and the dream of one day becoming a writer. Luckily, after a few failed career choices, she gets to follow that dream—writing down-to-earth contemporary romance and romantic suspense. From farmers to cowboys, Midwest to *the* West, Nicole writes stories about people finding themselves and finding love in the process. She lives in Missouri with her husband and two sons and dreams of someday owning a barn.

Books by Nicole Helm

Harlequin Intrigue

A North Star Novel Series

Summer Stalker
Shot Through the Heart
Mountainside Murder

A Badlands Cops Novel

South Dakota Showdown
Covert Complication
Backcountry Escape
Isolated Threat
Badlands Beware
Close Range Christmas

Carsons & Delaneys: Battle Tested

Wyoming Cowboy Marine
Wyoming Cowboy Sniper
Wyoming Cowboy Ranger
Wyoming Cowboy Bodyguard

Visit the Author Profile page at Harlequin.com.

CAST OF CHARACTERS

Sabrina Killian—North Star agent sent to the Tetons to track down a mysterious hit man. Instead, she finds his target, an avalanche and a mystery to solve.

Connor Lindstrom—A former navy SEAL currently working for a search and rescue team that operates in and around the Tetons in Wyoming. He's rescuing a hiker who's fallen over a cliff when a woman pretending to be a police officer tries to apprehend the victim. Connor's having none of it...until the victim disappears.

Froggy—Connor's search and rescue dog, trained to work in tracking, particularly lost hikers and during avalanches.

Iona—Connor's partner in search and rescue, who pilots the S&R helicopter when it's necessary for a rescue.

Holden Parker—A North Star agent and close friend of Sabrina's who helps Sabrina and Connor as they unravel the hit man mystery.

Nathan Averly—Connor's former navy SEAL buddy and the key to what connects Connor to the mysterious hit man. He currently lives in Montana at a rehabilitation facility due to injuries sustained during combat.

Shay—Current head of the mysterious North Star group, who hands out assignments and provides backup when necessary.

Chapter One

Sabrina Killian was *finally* free. The cast she'd been in for six weeks was off, and though she'd been ordered to take it easy, she had no plans to do so.

Not when there was *finally* an assignment to be accomplished.

Sabrina walked through the sprawling house that acted as North Star Group's headquarters. She knew Shay, the head of the group, and Elsie, lead on IT, had been working overtime to trace the dangerous weapons involved in their last successful mission. She expected this meeting to mean they'd made some progress.

She met Holden in the hallway to the conference room.

"You know it'll be me next. Shay's not sending you out on a mission when you're still banged up," Holden said, obnoxiously as always. It didn't matter that Holden was the reason she was here, and that she owed him…possibly her life, and surely her soul. She still liked to bicker with him.

After all, it was a bar fight that had led him to invite her to join North Star, instead of letting her wallow her failed life away on bar fights and bad elements. She'd helped bring down the gang she'd been considering joining up with. Because of Holden Parker.

She still gave him crap about his unwillingness to hit a girl, even when she could take it.

And boy, could Sabrina take it. She'd been *this* close to being one of the first female navy SEALs when a freak injury had ended her military career.

It might have ended her life if she hadn't happened to find fault with Holden Parker in a seedy bar in the middle of South Dakota. These days, she loved him like the big brother she'd never had, and she would never, ever admit that to him.

"We'll see," she muttered with a scowl.

"Hey, remember when I saved your butt a few weeks ago?" He slung his arm around her shoulder companionably.

She shrugged off the arm before giving him a fake saccharine sweet smile. "Hey, remember when I kicked your butt a few years ago? Besides, if you'd given me a little more time, I could have taken those guys on my own. Fractured arm and all." And she would have if Holden hadn't swept in trying to be a superhero.

She'd been ambushed by three brainless goons, and she'd been *this* close to taking all three of them when one had tripped her and she'd fallen wrong on her arm. It had incapacitated her, *briefly*, but she would have kicked their butts one-handed anyway. She knew it. Instead, Holden had taken care of it.

It still grated.

"Must be losing your touch. Want to try me now?"

Holden offered, spreading his arms as if to offer her a free punch.

She tossed her long, dark ponytail over her shoulder. "When you've hung up your warped moral code about hitting women who were *this* close to being navy SEALs, I'll fight you."

Before he could respond to that, someone cleared their throat.

"Children," Shay said blandly, standing in the entrance of the conference room, arms crossed. "If you'd enter so we could get this started?"

Sabrina sent Holden a haughty look, then sailed into the room in front of him. She took her usual chair and waited for Shay to come around to the front of the room. It was only her and Holden as field operatives in the meeting. Elsie sat at her computer in the corner tapping away.

It was weird without Reece. For two years now, it had been the three of them as the leads on all major missions. Shay always brought all three of them in to consult before she decided who to send.

Now, it was just Sabrina and Holden. Shay was going to have to promote one of the younger field operatives to take Reece's supervisory position so there was a trio again. But she hadn't yet.

Sabrina couldn't really blame her. There were some good options, but no one who'd been around nearly as long as Holden and her. Or Shay herself, who'd dedicated her life to North Star longer than any of them.

Sabrina *really* hoped she got this assignment. She was edgy and tired of being cooped up rehabilitating and thinking about all the changes North Star had been going through. She was a woman who needed to move, needed to act. Being injured and sitting around *thinking* suited her not at all.

"What we have in the wake of the whole situation from a few weeks ago is two highly dangerous weapons, in the hands of two highly dangerous individuals."

"So, let's go," Holden said.

"As if anything is that simple. From what our friends at the FBI can figure, we've just tangled with a highly specialized, complicated death machine."

"I thought it was a weapons dealer," Sabrina said with a frown. They'd taken down a group selling black market weapons to the wrong kind of people six weeks ago. She tested her arm. It felt weak, and she was still pissed a group of muscle-bound thugs had gotten the better of her, even if she would have been able to get herself out of that mess eventually.

It wouldn't happen again.

"Turns out, the weapons being supplied were only a small, tiny cog of a much bigger machine. Which means they'll just replace their weapons dealer. The FBI is putting a team on finding out more about this machine, but our job is much more urgent. While the FBI is trying to smoke out the head of the big group, we've got to stop two different hit men. Before we fully took down the weapons dealer group, they shipped off two untraceable, highly powered guns—and distributed them to two ghosts. And I do mean ghosts."

"Sounds like a challenge," Holden said, kicking

back in his chair and balancing it on two legs. Like Sabrina, Holden was always ready for a challenge.

"Two hit men. Two guns that can make a joke out of Kevlar. We don't know who the hit men are. We don't know who the targets are. We don't even know how much time we have before they act. We know nothing. Except the guns themselves. The first lead we've gotten, thanks to Elsie's tireless work, is the delivery of ammunition for our weapon to two different PO boxes. Each equally untraceable as the owners don't exist and security footage gives next to nothing away."

"So there's video of the ammunition being picked up?" Sabrina asked.

"Elsie's hacked what she can, and I'll show you that in a moment. Either way, you're going to split up and scout each address out. Our first target is Wilson, Wyoming. This is the only video we have of our suspect retrieving the package from the PO box."

A grainy security feed showed up on the big screen in front of them. A man dressed head to toe for the winter weather walked over to one of the boxes. He kept his head completely turned away from the camera, and he was wearing too many clothes to make any sort of defining characteristic out.

"A bit overdressed, isn't he?" Holden murmured.

"It's still cold enough at the upper elevations, but you're right. Seems odd. Especially since we know what's in the package. And what makes it more shady…" Shay nodded to Elsie and another grainy video clicked on thanks to her manning the computers in the corner.

This video was similarly set up to the first, but definitely a different post office. "Evening, Nebraska."

Another person, dressed a bit heavy for May, came in in much the same way the man from the earlier video had.

"That gives us two targets. I want you both on it. You can take a team if you want, but the first stages might be best done alone until you actually find the target. Though I'd want a team close by for backup. And a full team completely in place before you take action."

"Define full team," Holden replied with a wide grin.

"We've got two people, at least, about to be killed, for reasons unknown to us. That might only be the tip of the iceberg based on what I'm getting from the Feds. Either way, we have very little to go on. It's important. But it's not more important than your own lives."

"Don't you think that depends?" Sabrina asked, without fully thinking the words through.

Shay fixed her with a hard look. "This is a dangerous mission. You're risking your life by taking it on, but that doesn't mean you have to play hero."

"How would we live with ourselves if we didn't?" Holden asked, with none of his usual humor or joking.

Shay blinked, and Sabrina knew that something about Reece getting seriously shot last month, then leaving North Star to go live his happily-ever-after, had left Shay…altered. Sabrina would never call her boss *timid*, but there was something about her that seemed to think they were all more fragile.

Sabrina refused to be or feel fragile. She turned to

Holden, bypassing Shay all together. "You take Nebraska," they told each other simultaneously.

"Not a snowball's chance in flat prairie hell," Holden replied.

She dug a penny out of her pocket. "Flip for it?"

"Who carries change around?"

"I found it yesterday." *Find a penny, pick it up, and all day long you'll have good luck.* Silly saying, but she hadn't been able to ignore the fact she needed some luck. "Thought it'd be good luck. Come on. Call it in the air. You win, you choose where you want to go."

Holden shrugged and grinned. "Sure. You should know luck always falls down on my side."

She flipped the coin, and Holden called heads. When it landed tails, she feigned humble surprise. "Oh, dear. It looks like I get to pick, doesn't it?"

"All right. Sabrina, you're headed to the Tetons," Shay said, clearly trying to head off any arguing. "Holden, that means Nebraska for you."

The look on Holden's face was darn near comical. Confusion dawning into horror and denial.

Sabrina reached over and slapped him on the back. "Don't worry. I'll send you pictures of the mountains."

SHE DID IN fact text Holden pictures. Repeatedly. It brought her great joy as she canvassed the area where the ammunition had been shipped. She posed as a police officer and questioned the post office employees. She got a few leads, and the current one had her taking a good ten-mile hike up the side of a mountain.

She didn't mind. Better here than sitting in a car

at a dead end on Main Street, USA. She chuckled to herself, took a gorgeous picture of the sun rising over the mountains, purposefully cropping out the clouds that were quickly moving in. She sent it to Holden and added a *wish you were here. Oh, wait. No, I don't.*

She'd gone another mile or so when she got the text back.

I got a lead. $10 says I get my guy first.

We'll talk when you're confident enough to raise it to 50.

Which she wasn't. The plan had been to interview any hikers she found along the way to see if they'd seen the man she *thought* might be the suspect who'd gotten the ammunition from the PO box.

But the trail was mostly empty. *Odd for spring*, she thought. Then again she hadn't checked the weather forecast today as she had no plans of delaying following this guy. Maybe there was snow coming. She looked at the clouds quickly covering what little sunlight she had.

Maybe she'd get caught in a thunderstorm. She'd prefer the snow, but she'd deal with either. Weather wasn't going to stop her when she finally had a lead.

So, she hiked, and felt mildly comforted by the fact Holden hadn't texted back. Whatever his lead was, he was no more confident in it than she was in hers.

She was about halfway up the trail when she finally saw some people. A trio gathered around the edge of the cliff the trail currently skirted. Sabrina wondered if they saw wildlife or a pretty vista below.

They probably hadn't seen the man she was after if they were still on their way up, but on the off chance they were on their way down...

The faint sound of helicopter blades began to punctuate the air. Sabrina frowned up at the sky and then the people at the cliff. She moved toward them as the helicopter came into view, then was hidden behind trees and rock again.

Sabrina stood at the edge and looked down at where the people had their attention. A man was lying a good twenty feet below. He intermittently moaned and grabbed at his leg.

She couldn't decide if this was a boon or terrible timing that she was about ninety percent certain the man below was the man she was after. She'd have to wait for the SAR team to get him up here, then somehow convince the search and rescue guys she should get custody of the injured man. That was a challenge.

But she'd caught up to him.

"Everything all right?" Sabrina asked.

The woman next to her turned in surprise. She took her measure quickly. "We were hiking and heard someone moaning. We saw him down there and called the emergency number. Search and rescue is coming." She eyed Sabrina's pack. "Are you going up or coming down?"

"Up. You?"

"Same, or we were. Once the SAR team gets here, we're headed back. We just got word from our friends back at the resort that a nasty storm is coming through. Winds and snow. Avalanche warning, I guess. Isn't safe to hike here right now."

Sabrina didn't bother to hide her disappointment. Bad weather was going to cause her some problems.

She could tell the SAR helicopter had landed. There wasn't enough room on this part of the trail, but based on sheer noise, she'd say they had a spot not much farther up. She didn't know a thing about search and rescue, or how they'd get to the man below, but that wasn't her concern.

"Well, you and your friends should head back," Sabrina said, adopting a tone of authority.

The woman glanced worriedly at the two people she was with, older and not in as good shape. "We should, but I thought maybe the search and rescue team might need to talk to us."

"Did you see it? The fall, I mean."

"No, but—"

"Then you're good. But if you're worried you can leave your contact information with me." Sabrina flashed her fake badge. "I'm with the local PD. Off duty," she said pretending to be disappointed her time off was interrupted. "But I can handle it from here on your behalf. Wouldn't do having tourists stuck up here." Sabrina offered a friendly smile.

The woman's face lit up. "Oh, isn't that handy? Well, here." She showed Sabrina her phone and Sabrina took a picture of the number on it. "We're staying together in Jackson Hole. We'll be there through the week. Longer if the weather is as bad as they're predicting."

"We'll be in touch if we need to ask you any questions. Otherwise, you hurry back and enjoy the rest of your vacation."

"Oh, that's so great. Thank you."

The trio discussed then tramped off, disappearing around the curve of the trail just as a man and a woman with search and rescue gear appeared on the opposite side of the trail. Sabrina waved them over, and pointed to the man below.

"You made the call?" said the man, a tall, broad-shouldered...*god* was the word that came to Sabrina's mind, but no matter how good anyone looked, no man was a god. Most were barely human.

He had thick, light brown hair slightly poking out of a bright orange ski cap. He wore layers, but she could tell he was in just *fine* shape underneath. His eyes were the color of the sky, and his mouth...well, it was hard not to get a little fluttery over a soft mouth pressed into a grim line when a guy had a jaw like that.

"Uh, yeah, I made the call," Sabrina offered, looking away from the mouth and the jaw back to the man moaning below them. "I didn't see him fall. Don't know the guy. Just heard him moaning and saw he'd fallen. So I called the emergency number." Sabrina figured using the other woman's story as her own was good enough.

He got to work with his female partner. Ropes and pulleys and all sorts of things Sabrina didn't have much experience with. It was interesting though how it could all work together so that the man could rappel down the sheer face of a mountain certain all would hold his weight.

And the injured man below.

The partner and the man on the ropes spoke into little comm units much like the ones Sabrina might use with her team if they were moving in together on a target.

Sabrina watched from the edge of the mountain as the rescue guy strapped the injured man to a board. Sabrina still wasn't sure that was the man *she* was after, but it was the only lead she had.

She couldn't let this SAR team whisk the injured guy off to a helicopter and then to a hospital. Especially with a storm coming in. She had to stop this somehow.

By the time the SAR partners had pulled the man up to the trail, Sabrina had her plan.

"Not as injured as he seems to think," the SAR man was muttering to his partner as he started to unstrap the injured man.

But Sabrina watched the victim. He kept his gaze on the bonds on his legs and arms. There was calculation in his expression as one leg was freed. Like he had some kind of plan.

This was her guy. She didn't *know* it, but she *felt* it, and that was good enough for Sabrina. She marched forward, pulling out the fake badge again. "Excuse me." Sabrina stopped the SAR guy from unstrapping another restraint. "Police." She flashed the badge quickly in his face, hastily returning it to her pocket so he couldn't examine it. "I'm going to have to take it from—"

"Well, that's fake," the rescuer said, gesturing at her pocket.

Even though it *was*, Sabrina couldn't ignore the spurt of outrage that he'd seen through her quick flash of the badge. "Excuse me, I think—"

"Out of the way, miss."

But she would not *get out of the way.* She stood firm. "I'm afraid I can't let you transport him anywhere, *mister*. This man is a danger to society, and I'm in charge of—"

He stood, and though she was a tall woman, this SAR guy had a good few inches on her. And was all well-packed, *excellently* honed muscle. "You can take that up with him once we've transported him to the hospital."

"Can I see your badge?" the rescue woman asked, politely.

Sabrina glared at the dark-haired woman, noticed her partner was doing the same.

"It's fake," the guy said between clenched teeth. "I don't know why, and I don't care. You take whatever up with him once we've done our job and dropped him at the hospital."

"How do you know the badge is fake?" the woman whispered to the man.

SAR god held Sabrina's gaze, eyes cold and assessing. He crossed his *very* impressive arms across his chest. Seriously, Sabrina was going to have to get herself in need of being searched and rescued once this was all over.

But for now, she had a job to do. Whether he believed her fake badge or not. "The guy's mine. Thanks for rescuing him and all, but your job is done." Sabrina moved forward, sure the man wouldn't put up a fight.

But he stopped her. Bodily.

Sabrina's jaw dropped. "Did you just *touch* me?" She'd been spending too much time with Holden if that surprised her.

"I rescued him, as I was called to do. I'll continue to rescue him until I've finished the job. Again, I'll invite you to visit him at the hospital if you have some sort of actual official business. But as of now? I'd recommend getting the hell off this mountain before the storm blows in and I have to come and search and rescue *you*."

She had a half thought to grin at him and offer a far more enjoyable suggestion, but again, the assignment came first. If she got to the potential hit man now, she'd bet Holden that $50 for sure.

So, she'd just have to take the rescue dude out. Judging by the nervous woman next to him, she wasn't going to fight back. And they didn't have weapons, so Sabrina gave no warning, she struck out.

The man dodged her punch, immediately followed up with a grab that Sabrina ducked. They grappled like that, neither landing blows, and predicting the other's move right before the other did it.

They had the same moves. The same style.

Sabrina blew out an irritated breath and dropped her hands. "Oh, God, you're *military,* aren't you?"

He didn't relax or drop out of the fighting stance. "Same goes, huh?"

"You guys?" the woman said, her voice a little timid. "The fighting is a real meet cute and all, but our guy is gone."

Sabrina whirled at the same time the man did. The board was empty.

The SAR guy swore, furious blue eyes meeting her own furious ones. "You let him get away!" they shouted at each other.

"Iona," he barked to the woman he worked with. "Get in the helicopter and search. I'm taking it by foot." The woman immediately jogged away, but Sabrina wasn't done with this guy.

"I'm a police officer, and I—"

"And I'm Bigfoot, lady. I'm SAR, so I'll search and rescue and you can go off and lie to someone else."

He strode off, a big, broad-shouldered man with a foul temper. Yeah, he was *hot*.

But there was no way he was going to find her quarry first.

Chapter Two

Connor Lindstrom knew he hadn't gotten rid of the woman pretending to be a police officer. She was following the same tracks as he was. She held back so he couldn't see her, but he knew she was there all the same.

There and probably planning how she could get around him. Considering it was clear she had a military background, and likely a mind under all those lies, he figured she'd probably manage it.

But *his* job was to search, and to rescue. So, regardless of what was up with her, and what she wanted from their escapee—*his* job was rescue. Plain and simple. With the weather ready to turn, Connor had to work fast. Before this turned into a more complicated rescue than it already was.

The man he'd brought up from the cliff face had essentially escaped a rescue. It didn't sit right with Connor, but it wasn't his job to figure out why. Search. Rescue. The end.

He wished he had Froggy with him. She could run ahead and cut the guy off at the pass, but as it was, she was back at his cabin. Connor eyed the sky. Luckily he had a dog door in the back, because Froggy would need some cover before Connor managed to return.

"Are you sure about tracking him on foot?" Iona's voice crackled through his comm unit.

"Yup."

"The storm is going to be bad. If we get up—"

"Get the helicopter back to base. The guy wasn't hurt as bad as he was acting, so he could get a bit of a lead on us. I'll keep searching."

"Storm is coming, Con. You can't outrun it."

"Yeah, well, I know how to weather a storm. You drop the heli. If I need backup, I'll radio."

"I don't like this."

Connor eyed the sky again. No, he didn't like it either, but she didn't have time to argue with him about it. "Tough. Get in the air." Iona was a fine pilot and she'd get the helicopter back to base in one piece as long as she got off soon. For him, he'd survive whatever spring storm the Tetons threw at him and get to the man who'd...

Well, he hadn't been that injured. Connor had also noticed a few ropes on the cliff below the one he'd rapelled onto. Had the man been doing some rappelling of his own? And this woman after him. Military? Former military?

It made his back itch, between his shoulder blades, where no good feelings ever settled. Mostly, he'd like to pretend to ignore the woman's existence. Do his job and disappear, never to have those sharp brown eyes vaguely mocking him again.

He grunted irritably. There was no use pretending she wasn't there. Somewhere. "Are you really going to follow me the whole time?" he called out.

She appeared, off to his right. She was closer than he'd thought she'd be, he'd give her that. Tall, slim, but the way she walked, moved and tried to fight him— it all spoke to a muscular body underneath the warm hiking layers.

Probably shouldn't be thinking about that.

"I know your job is rescue," she said, flicking a thick black braid over her shoulder. She should be wearing a hat and gloves, but wasn't and didn't seem worse for the wear over it.

She would. Once the storm hit.

"But my job is stopping this guy. So, you could just leave off. Jump in the helicopter. Let me…"

She trailed off as the sounds of the helicopter pulsed through the air, then its body became visible. Iona taking it back to base. *Thank God.*

"No such luck, lady."

The woman scowled and shoved her hands into the pockets of her coat. She wore dark, drab colors but there was something about her that was a bit like a beacon. Maybe it was because of the snow around them, the brightness still holding on against the incoming clouds. She was the opposite of all that. Dark. Quiet. Sharp like a blade.

Except there was an *energy* about her, pumping off of her. Much like the impending storm, she looked determined to cause some damage. She hiked right next to him, matching him stride for stride. Her profile was strong, her eyes stubborn. There'd be no getting rid of her.

But there'd be no getting rid of him either. He saw the job through. Always.

As if she sensed that, she blew out a breath. "So, how about this? He's a hit man. A highly trained hit man, equipped with some nasty gun and ammo that can rip up Kevlar. Still want to rescue him?"

Connor didn't even pause to think it over. "It's my job. You know what's *not* my job? Believing anything you say." Though he wondered if she might at least be telling part of the truth. *She* didn't need to know he thought that though.

"But you know as well as I do that he wasn't as hurt as he was pretending. There were ropes he'd dropped and tried to hide. The dude was faking it."

So she'd noticed those details too. "If he's so bad, and so dangerous, why are you following him? Alone?"

"Because I'm so bad and so dangerous too, baby." She flashed a grin at him.

He almost believed her, and that was…uncomfortable. "You're not armed."

She raised an eyebrow, following him up the side of the rock—clearly not worried about going off trail. "Think again."

Connor would have, but he realized the direction the man's tracks were taking them. The moron had gone in about the worst direction possible. He pulled up off the rock and onto a long sheet of snow and ice. The tracks continued up.

"He's heading for high ground," the woman said.

"To get a shot off," she murmured, coming to stand next to him again. "Hit man, remember?"

Connor'd give her credit, that was the only reason he could think of someone would head this way, alone, and in this weather. Unless someone was completely lost. But… "He didn't have anything on him. I would have seen it. Felt it when strapping him to the board."

"Doesn't mean a weapon, specifically his gun, isn't hiding somewhere. Cave? Buried? I sure wouldn't climb up that unless I had a really, *really* good reason."

"Who's he going to shoot out here?"

"I wouldn't know. But I know I'm going to stop him."

Connor would have questioned her, but the shift in the wind had his internal senses going off. He stopped abruptly. When she made another step and he *heard* the hollow echo of it, he began to see the cracks. The danger.

"Stop," he ordered, quietly but with enough gravity to have her doing just that.

"What is it?" she demanded.

"We have to get out of here. And not the way you came."

"Why?"

He sized her up, how far they had to the beginning of the trail. Nope, he'd have to take her with him. And fast. "I don't particularly want to be buried alive in an avalanche, that's why."

SABRINA WOULDN'T SAY she was *scared* exactly. She was tough. She could survive.

She just didn't think surviving an avalanche sounded

like a lot of fun. It was a step above being taken out by a sniper though.

So, when the man moved quickly, she followed. He scooted down the mountain, and then she began to hear what she thought maybe he'd heard back there that had made him stop. An odd, hollow echoing every time their footsteps landed on the snow.

"Pick up the pace, or you're going to be buried."

"I'm *right* behind you."

He all but leaped from one rocky surface to another and Sabrina paused for half a second, maybe. With the cold and the jump, she was in danger of re-injuring her hip—the whole reason she was here rather than on some military mission as a SEAL.

Here was better. At first, she'd only told herself that, only *tried* to make herself believe that because the one thing she'd wanted in the world had been taken away from her in a freak accident that had shattered her hip six years ago.

She took the jump, and though she felt the twinge, nothing broke, nothing shattered. No time to be grateful for it. She broke into a jog to keep up with mister SAR.

Here was better. She repeated it to herself as everything about the man in front of her *screamed* military, and she felt a bit like she was back in BUDs training, desperately trying to prove herself.

Here was better. She believed it now. Most days. There was a freedom to being part of North Star. She got to have her own life, make friends and not constantly have to prove herself as the only woman in the field—considering her current boss was a woman. She loved what she did, loved what she'd done.

She'd had a part in taking down a huge and dangerous biker gang. Now, she was going to get that hit man.

Once she survived what she could only assume was the beginning of an avalanche. She glanced behind them briefly and found it freezing her in place.

She saw the snow simply *move*, a huge big sheet of it.

The man she'd been running with grabbed her arm and jerked her through the haze of unadulterated fear to look away from the huge piles of snow getting ready to unload on them. He pointed to a little dot a ways away. "That's our target. Just run. Do *not* look back."

He moved, so she followed doing what he said. Just ran. Didn't look back. Of course, she desperately wanted to, but she could hear the crackling of nothing good. The wind howled. A freezing rain started to fall, pelting her face with stinging cold.

Still, she ran, until the dot became clearer and clearer as a small cabin. Wouldn't that cabin just be swallowed up by the snow too?

But, much as she didn't trust anyone, she trusted a SAR guy to know where to go to not get buried alive by an avalanche.

Her breath puffed painfully in and out of her lungs, the air so cold it felt like knives everywhere it touched.

They were almost to the cabin and Sabrina couldn't help it. She looked behind her and the big wall of snow…

"Do you have a death wish?" the guy yelled above the din of storm and avalanche.

She hadn't stopped running, so she didn't think the look behind was *that* bad. Except for the terror that had invaded her at the sight of what was bearing down on them. Still she kept up with him and noticed there was an odd triangular stone structure behind the cabin. Would that keep them from being buried alive in the cabin?

She didn't have the breath to ask, so she simply ran with him all the way into the tiny cabin.

It was warmer inside, though not expressly *warm*. They both stood inside, breathing raggedly. Sabrina couldn't get a sense of her surroundings at first. She was too busy trying to catch her breath, trying to weather the weakness that had flooded her after she had been an idiot and looked back despite his warnings.

She heard the roar, the *thumps*. But the cabin didn't shudder or shake or come apart around them like she half expected.

She wasn't sure how long they stood there, panting and not saying anything. It gave her some gratification that it was taking him as long as her to be able to breathe normally again.

When she had some wits about her, she looked around the room. It was spartan. A stone fireplace, a couch and a rug. No artwork on the walls. A few books piled up on the floor in the corner.

A big dog, a silky golden retriever, padded into the room from somewhere deeper in the cabin. It gave Sabrina one look then let out a low *woof*.

"Froggy. Sit," the man ordered through deep breaths.

Froggy. Everything inside of Sabrina recoiled as she eyed the man with disgust. "Oh. God. You *were* a navy SEAL," she muttered. Figured of all the dang people to get stuck in an avalanche with, she'd be trapped with a damn *SEAL*.

Connor raised an eyebrow. "Something against SEALs specifically?"

"Yeah. Specifically." She gestured to the outside, wanting to change the subject. "We going to be buried alive in here or what?"

"Or what. Deflection wedge should keep us safe."

"Should?"

He shrugged, and walked over to the fireplace. He began to build a fire as his dog walked over to where he crouched and curled up on the rug.

"What now?" Sabrina demanded.

"We wait until it's safe. Then you go back to whatever hellhole you crawled out of, and Froggy and me here go save your friend."

"He's a dangerous assassin."

"Yeah, well, for all I know, he's dead as a doornail. But we'll find him, one way or another." He stood, the fire crackling away. He shrugged out of his coat and *yowza.*

Underneath he wore a heavy sweatshirt, likely over another layer. Thermal probably. But *dang* the guy had a set of shoulders on him.

Navy SEAL, remember? You hate those.

She did. A lot. Didn't mean she couldn't enjoy appreciating the hardware, did it?

He strode out of the room, so Sabrina followed. She was trailing wet tracks through his house, but then again, so was he, so she didn't feel too bad.

He walked into another room, a small, cozy kitchen. Off the kitchen was another tinier room where he hung his coat. He pulled off the comm unit he'd had attached to it, then spoke into it, still saying nothing to her.

"Iona. Copy?"

"You okay? That came out of nowhere, huh?" the woman—the pilot—said in return over the unit. She seemed very…casual about an avalanche and a guy being caught out in it.

Sabrina supposed that was their job. To be calm and casual about what they did. She understood that, certainly.

"I'm good. At my cabin. We'll give it time to settle, then Froggy and I will head out and try to find our target."

"What about the woman?"

The man looked back at her, scowling. "She's with me. I plan on getting her out of my hair ASAP."

Sabrina smiled sweetly at him. "Good luck with that, sailor."

Chapter Three

Connor was hardly surprised this woman was going to be difficult. She practically had *pain in the butt* stamped across her forehead.

"I'll let you know when I head out again," Connor said into the unit, then turned to face the woman currently screwing with all his plans. This tall, mouthy stranger dripping in his kitchen.

"You're going to want to take all that off."

She fluttered her eyelashes on him. "Don't you think you should at least give me your name first?"

A nameless hookup wasn't his style. It didn't appeal. Or at least, it usually didn't. Still, he didn't mind using her own tactics on her. He smiled. "Some of us have work to do, *baby*."

She didn't scowl exactly, but her fake flirtatious expression got harder. "You can search and rescue all you want, but that guy is mine. I don't rest, or leave you be, until I've got him."

"You're not going to leave me be? Well, that *is* a threat." He moved past her and down the short hall to his bedroom. She followed, because of course she followed. He pulled the sweatshirt off. The freezing rain hadn't penetrated his waterproof coat, but the run and all the layers had caused him to work up a sweat. He needed warm, dry clothes fit for an avalanche rescue as that would be next on the agenda. Once the most dangerous part of the snow pile-up had settled.

She hadn't entered his room, but she leaned in his doorway, arms folded over her chest, one ankle crossed over the other. *Dripping* on his hardwood floor.

He sighed. "Do you mind?"

She raised her eyebrows all faux innocence. "I don't mind at *all*. Might be quite a nice show. I enjoy a good show."

He shook his head, appalled he wanted to laugh at her brazenness. "You've got to be freezing," he muttered.

"I've survived worse."

"Haven't we all." He jerked a drawer open, found a dry Henley and tossed it at her. Then went pawing through the next drawer for a pair of sweats and threw those in her direction too. "Bathroom is at the end of the hall. Change. We'll throw your gear into the dryer, then decide what's next."

"I know what's next. I—"

He simply walked over to her leaning in his doorway, gave her a gentle thrust backward, then closed the door in her face. Locked it for good measure.

He was half convinced she'd knock it down, except there was nothing but silence on the other side of the door, then the sound of footsteps retreating.

It gave him the chance to change completely, and

put on a fresh pair of boots. It gave him a chance to *breathe*.

He didn't know what she was. Not a cop. Maybe some kind of mercenary. Not unheard-of for someone to leave the military and use their skills to go that route. But her excuse was that she was looking for a hit man. Though he supposed mercenaries didn't have to always be looking to do harm. Maybe she was the kind that hunted down the bad.

If he believed her story. Unfortunately, what she'd told him matched with the way his rescue escapee behaved. Except why here? The Tetons might be well visited, but he hadn't picked a busy trail or the part of the park closer to Jackson Hole and its never-ending spate of tourists.

Didn't add up, and Connor really hated when things didn't add up.

But that had to come secondary to the task at hand, which was a post-avalanche rescue. *If* there was a guy to save after the avalanche.

Fully dressed, Connor moved back into the kitchen. He tried to forget about the woman in his cabin as he made coffee, got out one of his print maps and turned the emergency radio on. Froggy curled up under the table he worked at while Connor made notes, got himself some coffee and formulated a plan. He glanced at the time and knew loss of daylight would be the biggest challenge.

He looked up as she entered his kitchen. This strange woman in his clothes, holding a dripping mass of her own. Something he refused to identify tightened in his gut.

"Dryer's back through there," he said, nodding his head toward the utility room off the kitchen.

She nodded and disappeared. When she returned, he tried to pretend she wasn't there, but he just couldn't manage it with all that *energy* pumping off her. She'd unbraided her hair, and it was still damp, but she must have run a towel through it because she wasn't dripping anymore.

"You got any extra mugs, or do I have to drink that right out of the pot?" she asked with a nod toward the coffeemaker.

"Please, make yourself at home. You're a guest after all," he said, sarcasm dripping from every word.

She laughed, low and smoky. "In that case," she said, opening the wrong cupboard, "I'll just poke around until I find what I want."

"Fantastic," Connor muttered. He didn't bother telling her what cabinet the mugs were in. She'd probably just open them all even if she knew.

So, he focused on his map and left her to it. When she slid into the other chair at his kitchen table, he had to fight back a grimace.

He really preferred to be alone.

"Sabrina," she said, out of nowhere.

He blinked and looked up at her. "Huh?"

"My name is Sabrina. So while you're inwardly cursing me, you've at least got a name to go along with it. Now yours? I want to inwardly curse you, too."

Again, he wanted to laugh. But there was no way he was going to let himself. "Connor."

"Connor the navy SEAL."

"Former navy SEAL," he amended, going ahead and flipping off the radio since she was apparently going to *chat* now. Iona or someone at base would notify him when it was safe to go out.

"Little young to be former, aren't you?"

He lifted his gaze to hers. "I assume you're former *some* kind of military. Aren't you calling the kettle black?"

She kicked back in her chair. "So, injury then?"

Didn't he wish. But that was the cover. "Yeah, injury. You too?"

She nodded.

"Yet here you are outrunning avalanches and allegedly chasing down the bad guys, without so much as a limp."

She raised both hands. "You can take the gal out of the military…"

There was more to her story. He could tell by the steely glint in her eye, the way her entire posture had gone a little rigid, like she was ready to fight something off.

But it was none of his business, and he didn't want it to be.

"Look, lady. Avalanche rescue is serious work. You—"

"Sabrina. Not to be a cliche, but I ain't no lady."

Connor rolled his eyes. "Look—"

"Gotta make a call." She pushed away from the table and walked out of the room.

Connor allowed himself the full-on scowl. How he'd gotten saddled with her was beyond him. He could lose her. Here, or on the trail. He knew how to disappear. A man like him had to know how to disappear.

It was what he *should* do. But he had the sinking suspicion it wasn't what he'd end up doing.

SABRINA STEPPED OUT of Connor's cabin and onto a small porch covered in snow. The whole *world* was covered in snow. The white was nearly *blinding*, but the little stone triangle thing had kept Connor's cabin from being buried. They were surrounded on all sides by walls of snow, except this little front area. It was like being in an igloo.

Interesting. Except Sabrina had no clue how they were going to get out of here, surrounded by walls of snow and mountain debris, but she figured she'd trust Connor to figure that out. She didn't trust *people* as a rule, but she knew when to trust someone's skills.

Sabrina pulled out her phone and dialed Shay.

"Shay—" Shay answered the phone in something of an irritable bark.

"Well, things got interesting on my end. You sound annoyed."

"Yeah, that's a word for it. Holden got a lead, now he's MIA and I might hunt him down and take him out myself."

Sabrina's chest clutched in alarm, but she kept her voice steady. "How MIA?"

"It hasn't been long enough to worry," Shay said, calmer now.

But you're worried, Sabrina wanted to say. She held her tongue though. Shay was one of the few people in this world she'd do it for.

"I'm just irritated because if I know that brainiac he's done something stupid like turn off his phone. He'll pop up before the allotted time, probably with some new, good lead, and I won't be able to curse at him."

"You'll let me know when it is long enough to worry?"

Shay sighed. "You've got your own mission. Let's focus on that. Fill me in."

Sabrina had to stop herself from asking more questions about Holden's lead. About what trouble he might have gotten himself into. Shay was right. She had her own mission.

That you'd leave in a heartbeat to save Holden, given the chance.

True enough. Holden had given her a life by bringing her into the fold of North Star. She thought he might be the only man who'd cared about her without wanting to get in her pants, and that was…sacred.

But she had a mission in the here and now, and there was no way a woman survived being a North Star agent by being distracted. She filled Shay in on her day, where she was now, what the plan was.

"Former navy SEAL and current SAR," Shay said, her tone considering. "Well, not a bad partner to have, all things considered."

"I haven't told him anything. He didn't buy the cop

story, but I can probably make something up about being a bounty hunter or whatever."

"Good."

"He's *hot.*"

Shay snorted out a laugh, as had been Sabrina's hope. Levity had its place, and ever since Shay had become leader of North Star, she'd lost that. Sabrina knew Holden thought it was the pressure of the job, but Sabrina had always figured it laid on Shay more like guilt.

What she was guilty over, Sabrina didn't know.

"I'd worry about that," Shay said blandly, "but I know how you feel about military guys."

"Regardless, I won't quit until the job is done. He's in there poring over maps and whatnot, so I imagine we'll head out soon. Might not get back on messages right away while we're hiking. So, don't worry about me if I go radio silent."

"All right. Be careful. Don't fall for any hot military guys. Losing Reece was bad enough."

"You're stuck with me for the long haul." Sabrina hesitated before ending the call. "Even if I don't answer, give me a heads-up when Holden's accounted for."

"Will do. Take care of yourself. Check in when you can."

"Roger." Sabrina ended the call. She squinted out at all that blinding white. She couldn't worry about Holden when she had her own mission to attend to, but she gave herself a minute to worry, to think of him, and to hope he was okay.

Then she turned back into the cabin and left it behind. Right now, the only thing she could think about was hunting down her quarry before he killed whoever his target was.

Maybe he was buried under a pile of snow and rock, but Sabrina didn't think there was any way she was going to be that lucky.

When she entered the kitchen, Connor had cleaned up everything. He had two packs on the kitchen table—one of them was the one she'd been wearing earlier. There were some new supplies stacked up next to it.

The man in question was crouched eye-to-eye with the dog, murmuring sweet nothings.

Something in her stomach did a strange roll. It wasn't the lust thing. It was something softer, wistful almost. Which meant she was going to ignore it. Hardcore.

He stood slowly, staring at her, a mix of disgust and glare in his expression. "All right," he said on a sigh she might have told him was a bit dramatic if he didn't keep speaking. "I'd tell you that you can't come with me, but I'm not stupid enough to think you'd be smart enough to listen. Then I'd likely have to save your butt and I'm not in the mood to dig two people out of an avalanche. So, you'll follow along and do as I say. And before you argue, understand that if you get in my way, I can have you arrested."

"I do really bad with threats, hotshot. Really bad."

"And I do really bad with mouthy pains in the butt. I didn't ask for you to join me on a mission, but here we are."

She laughed, couldn't help it. There was something about his dry give-and-take that amused her. "All right, Con. Here's the deal. I'll follow the rules and instructions the entire time we're out there, up until we get the guy. Once he's free and good, I'll fight you for him." She held out a hand. "Deal?"

Connor heaved out a sigh. "Fine," he muttered, and shook her hand.

When she tried to pull her hand away, his grip tightened. "But if you break that deal, I'm having you arrested."

She thought about lifting up on her toes and pressing her mouth to his, just to see what he'd do. But if she was honest with herself, she was a little afraid of what *she* might do.

"One thing you're going to learn about me, Mr. navy SEAL, I keep my word." And she would. But that didn't mean she couldn't continue to be a pain in the butt *while* keeping her word.

Chapter Four

Connor double-checked his pack, ordered Sabrina to add the supplies he'd set out to hers. He checked in with Iona, then attached Froggy's special harness for avalanche rescue onto the dog. The bright orange-and-black harness allowed for leash attachments, including a load-bearing harness in case they should need to do another high line rescue.

Connor didn't like the fact that his job involved people being in danger, but he did love the act of his job. Even more than he'd enjoyed being a navy SEAL. While he'd joined the military to serve his country, to put his strength and discipline to the test, much of the actual real-life stuff he'd encountered hadn't been so cleanly about *helping* people.

War and conflict were gray areas and death and bureaucratic red tape and unfairness complicated all of that. Search and rescue were simple. You did the job. Sometimes you saved the day. Sometimes you didn't. But he didn't have to suffer a lot of deep personal moral dilemmas. Things were success or failure. He liked the black and white of it.

"Doesn't the dog get cold?" the woman—Sabrina—asked.

He was having a hard time thinking of her as *Sabrina*. She was all sharp edges and brash grins with the occasional innuendo tossed in for good measure. Sabrina seemed like a name better suited to someone… proper. Feminine. This woman looked like a slim, honed weapon in his Henley and the sweatpants that bagged on her. She was pure energy.

It was a shame he liked that in a woman.

"Froggy's fur keeps her warm," he said, running a hand over the dog's back. "The gear helps. She's trained for this, and as her handler and partner I pay attention to how she's faring. If the search goes on too long, we'll call for backup—both in terms of handlers *and* dogs."

"I'd like to avoid that."

So would he, but he wasn't going to let her know that. He shrugged negligently. "Search and rescue is rooted in *safety* for all involved. Searchers, dogs, victims. Everyone's well-being is taken into account. Because the whole principle behind it is *rescue*. Not creating bigger problems."

Sabrina pretended to yawn. It should offend him. Instead he had to stifle a grin.

He needed to get this guy saved and fast so this strange woman would be out of his hair. For good.

"You'll need to put your clothes back on now that they're dry. I dumped them in the bathroom with some other stuff you'll want to wear. I've got your boots in the dryer. So, they'll be last."

"Awfully bossy."

"Yeah, well, I'm the boss. If this is going to go smoothly you might as well get used to it."

"If you're expecting a 'yes, sir' you read the room way wrong, babe."

"And if you think I'm going to get all flustered every time you *babe* me, you read the room wrong, sweetheart."

"Oh, come on, you can't honestly call me sweetheart with a straight face." She flashed him a grin and sauntered down the hallway with one last simmering look over her shoulder before she disappeared into his bathroom.

He really didn't want to like her. She was in his way, after all, but it was hard not to admire a woman with that much...*personality.*

When she finally came out, she'd put her own clothes back on, plus a few of the layers he'd thrown in there.

"You'll have to wear one of my coats. And a hat. And gloves. Who goes hiking in the cold without a hat and gloves?" He moved into the mudroom to gather the rest of the supplies he'd collected for her.

"My mistake, not planning for an avalanche."

"It was, yes," he agreed, handing her the coat, hat, gloves. She shrugged into the gear without complaint. They were a little big on her, but she was tall enough that the apparel wasn't swimming on her body. "A smart hiker checks the weather forecast, the potential for danger."

"I ain't no hiker. I'm—" She stopped herself, the first flicker of annoyance aimed at herself rather than him.

It was a kind of triumph, to Connor's way of thinking. Any time he could make this woman off balance enough to almost reveal some information, maybe he could understand what she was getting him roped into.

Connor opened the dryer and tested out her boots. "They'll do." He tossed them at her.

She shoved her feet into them, and he waited impatiently for her to lace them up. When she stood there after she was finished, he rolled his eyes. "The gloves. Unless you like frostbite."

"Okay, dad." She pulled the gloves on. "We ready yet? Or is it policy to let the guy suffocate?"

"Safety is the policy. The end."

"Damn, that's *so* hot."

"I don't have to take you along with me. You realize that, right?"

"But I'd go anyway. As you said yourself, that would only lead to you having to rescue me too. So, really, I'm doing you a favor."

Connor could not fully believe she was somehow spinning it that way, but she looked so pleased with herself, clearly she believed it. "God help me," he muttered, heading for the front door.

She trailed along much like Froggy did. Outside everything was the blinding white he'd expected. It was going to be a hell of a hike back to where they'd left any signs of their guy.

"You going to spill the reason you're after this dude?" he asked, marching through the snow as he eyed the sun through his sunglasses. They only had a few hours to get this accomplished before dark hindered their efforts. Iona would be putting together a night team, but Connor wanted this done, and Sabrina out of everyone's hair.

"I already did," Sabrina replied, squinting against the sun. "Bad guy with a bad gun, recall?"

He grumbled irritably to himself then dug a pair of sunglasses out of his pack and handed them to her. "You told me maybe half of why someone's after him, but you didn't tell me why you, specifically, are ineffectually tramping around mountains trying to…what, kill him?"

"I'm going to ignore the fact you said 'ineffectually tramping' because you're a guy and so obviously operating on half a brain. But for your information he's the hit man. Not me."

"That doesn't answer my question."

"I wasn't planning on answering your question."

"You know, I could hike you around, ditch you and leave you to the elements if I really wanted to. It wouldn't be hard." It was a threat he'd never act on, but maybe she wouldn't know that.

She snorted, clearly not taking him seriously. "You aren't the only one who went through navy SEAL training. I know how to survive."

SABRINA *REALLY* WISHED she hadn't said that. She had a mouth on her, so she was used to things flying out of it that she hadn't planned on, but she tried to keep personal stuff on the down low.

The way he stopped, turned and stared at her with his eyes wide, mouth open, she wanted to hunch away from his reaction. Instead, she lifted her chin at him. "What?" she demanded.

"You're Brina Killian."

She paled. No one had called her Brina in years. She'd left her nickname behind when she'd had to give up her SEAL dreams. She tried to fight off the cold slither of dread that worked its way up her spine. Tried to be smart in the face of swamping emotion.

There were a couple ways she could play it. Deny it. Admit it, flippantly. But the fact he knew her, or knew *of* her, was something she had to get to the bottom of. "How do you know that?"

"You shattered your hip." He eyed her suspiciously. "Healed up okay."

"Eventually. And I'll repeat myself. How do you know that?"

"Nathan Averly ring any bells?"

This time Sabrina didn't just blink in shock, she was pretty sure she blushed. "What about him?" Sabrina knew how small the military world could be, but the fact that this guy knew the ex-boyfriend that she hadn't treated all that well in the aftermath of her injury was…well, quite the twist of fate.

Shouldn't you be used to the cruel whims of chance by now?

"We were in a unit together. Came out the same time. He mentioned you."

"Super."

Connor went back to hiking, thank God. She could focus on moving her way through the high, hard-packed snow. Not on anything to do with an old life she hadn't just left behind, she'd forgotten all about. Purposefully.

She shook her head at herself. Sometimes a woman could lie to herself, but sometimes it didn't actually do any good. "Where is old Nate if not navy SEALing his way through life?"

Connor shrugged. "Not sure. Lost touch."

Sabrina opened her mouth to tell him he was lying, and that he was bad at it. But she thought better of it. Maybe she didn't want to know what had happened to Nate. Ignorance could absolutely be bliss. Especially when it came to old flames she'd done wrong.

They trekked in silence. Sabrina paid more attention to the dog than the man in front of her. Both because she was fascinated that a dog could have such an important job, and because she knew staring at Connor's backside was not good for her decision-making.

She wasn't sure how long they walked before Connor stopped and crouched next to the dog. He murmured something to the retriever. The demeanor in the dog changed, sharpened. Like she'd just gotten orders.

Sabrina looked around. Everything was still white. She got the sense they'd gone up in elevation, but mostly everything looked the same here as it had back at Connor's cabin.

The dog took the lead now, Connor following her, Sabrina behind him. Connor didn't look back to see if she was following him. Maybe he knew instinctually that she was. That she would.

"Wish I'd gotten Nebraska after all," she muttered to herself.

"What about Nebraska?" Connor asked, clearly more to annoy her than because he cared.

"Don't worry about it."

"The only thing I'm worried about is if you can really hack this."

She tried to keep the snap out of her voice since she knew he was purposefully needling her. "Do I sound winded?"

"Nate made that injury sound pretty major."

Go figure Nate would be haunting her still. "It was. It was also years ago. Injuries heal."

"Most major ones leave scars."

He had *no* idea. She also got an idea of what he was trying to do now. Irritate her with other topics so she'd answer his questions. But North Star was not public knowledge. Her personal involvement with the group even less so.

Back when Granger MacMillan had run the group, you got four years tops, then were a goner. If anyone ever made you, or you told someone about your job, you were out. The only one who'd ever gotten around that edict had been Shay herself.

Sabrina had respected Granger, but Shay loosening the stringent requirements of involvement in North Star, *and* how long a person could stay active in North Star, certainly made her future a lot more secure.

No one could get her kicked out of North Star except herself. Even with an injury she could transfer to some kind of intel job. She liked having that kind of control.

She thought about Shay's call earlier, and Holden, and pulled her phone out of her pocket.

"You won't get reception out here," Connor informed her.

She smirked at his back. Showed what he knew. Still, there were no messages. So Holden was still MIA. She slid her phone back into her pocket and pictured herself shoving her worry about Holden into its own compartment.

She had to focus on the task at hand. If she got this guy today, before the sun went down, she could be in Nebraska helping Holden by tomorrow.

She used that as fuel. It kept her hiking despite the way the cold bit into her. It kept her from snarking at Connor just for the sake of it. Focused. Determined. She'd get the job done.

She was starting to *feel* the elevation change, the way the air got thinner. "Are we higher than we were to start?"

"Yeah, but he was going up when the avalanche started. So, makes sense."

She wasn't convinced. Something about the tone in his voice had her wondering if he was lying to her. Whether for the sake of it or for some other reason, she didn't know.

It was when Connor paused to take a swig of his water bottle that Sabrina started to feel…exposed. She couldn't have said why. Just a tingling at the base of her neck, a heavy, throbbing *wrongness* to the still, the quiet and how completely open they were. An easy, easy target. "We need to get out of this open space. Now."

Connor scoffed. *Scoffed.* "There's no way someone somehow survived that avalanche *and* got a gun *and*—"

Sabrina could have let him go on with his *and*s, with his reasonable responses, but she had her gut feeling, and she went with it. She gave him a shove, and stuck her foot in just the right place to trip him in the force of her shove. Then launched her body so she'd land on top of him.

The gunshot ringing through the eerie silence before they'd fully hit the hard-packed snow beneath them was a relief. Her instincts were still always right on target.

"Told you," she muttered into the snow around them.

Chapter Five

It took Connor a few seconds to fully grasp what had just happened.

She'd been right. She may have even saved his life, pushing him out of the way, though he wasn't sure where the bullet landed and therefore what or who the presumed target was.

She'd been *right* either way. Connor had to sit with the fact that he'd…lost his touch. There'd been a time he could have sniffed something like that out. He would have felt it. Predicted it.

Maybe instead of being horrified he should be relieved. He'd left the navy SEALs feeling like a hunted dog. In the few years he'd been here he'd let that feeling go. Convinced himself his mountain was safe.

Now, it wasn't.

He thought of Nate, who'd never found that safe feeling. Who'd let that hunted feeling rule his life. Strange, the zigs and zags of this. His connection to Nate. Her.

No more shots rang out, though Sabrina stayed awkwardly splayed over the top of him. Like *she* was protecting *him*. He nudged her off of him, though made sure he kept her in the small hole they'd made in the snow—the force of their bodies making enough of an indentation in the hard pack.

Froggy sat, waiting for orders, as he and Sabrina thought about what the next move was.

The snow wouldn't protect them from gunfire, but if they stayed low enough, it might prevent the gunman from a good angle—depending on where the person was.

"If you wanted me underneath you, you could have asked," he said, because otherwise he was afraid he might thank her. He wasn't sure his pride could take the beating this woman would dole out if he *thanked* her.

"Ha. Ha. Maybe next time you'll listen to me. Or thank me for saving your life."

"How do you know he was shooting at me? Maybe he's shooting at the woman after him."

"Maybe," she muttered somewhat distractedly. "You got any binoculars in these packs?"

He rummaged around for them then handed them to her. She poked her head slightly above the edge of snowpack hiding them. Connor scanned the world around them. Wide open space here, with a big sheet of snow-covered rock to the west. That's where the shot had to have come from.

It was where Sabrina trained the binoculars. She looked out of them for what felt like several minutes, but he didn't rush her.

It had been a long time since he'd been on a military mission, but that's exactly what this felt like. Sniper. Interminable waiting in uncomfortable conditions. Teamwork that meant a little bit more because both of your lives were at stake.

Even if he hadn't predicted it. Even if his instincts had failed him. *This* felt right. It fit like an old glove. No matter how long it had been, he knew how to be the hunted. He knew how to fight it.

"Gone. Running or hiding." Sabrina made a considering sound before handing the binoculars back to him. "I think he'd have taken us both out if he'd hit one of us."

Connor noted she wasn't calling him the specific target, so she'd taken his point to heart. Surprising.

"But since he missed, thanks to me, he didn't want to stick around and risk getting caught?" She shook her head. "Not sure that makes sense, but not sure it doesn't."

"I'm not going to thank you."

"Then don't." She shrugged, surprisingly casual about the whole thing. "Just admit that my superior intelligence saved your very nice butt."

He snorted. "Did you just call my ass *nice* after getting shot at?"

She shrugged, humor lifting some of the gravity in her expression. "You could probably make a case for spectacular, but hard to tell with all those layers."

"You are something else," he muttered, irritated with her for being…something else, and irritated with himself for feeling a bit flustered. This was not a time to short-circuit.

"Look, I know what you're going to say to this and all, but I've got to give it my best shot. This guy is dangerous. Doesn't need rescuing. Go back to your cabin. Give this one up. I'll handle it, because he's my job. You don't need to make him yours."

She was serious. Not trying to poke at him. Not flashing her humor or sexual innuendo as some kind of weapon. No, this was a soldier. Through and through.

Harder to pretend or argue with a straight-forward woman just trying to get the job done—whatever her job happened to be.

Connor looked up at the rock face in front of them. He knew it would bother her, but he took his own time searching the place the gunman would have been with the binoculars.

No, there was no one visibly up there right now, but that didn't mean someone wasn't hiding. Hiding or running, either way, he and Sabrina wouldn't be able to pinpoint where he'd gotten the shot off. No matter what her skills were, she needed more than just her sharp brain and determination.

Froggy might be able to help with a search, but there were a few other options to exhaust before he went that route. "It might not be the same guy."

Sabrina gave him a doleful look, and he could hardly blame her. Of course it was the same guy. No one else would have been up on that mountain. Still, he'd had to offer the slim chance the two events of today were unrelated.

Less than unlikely. More and more, her dangerous hit man story held water. Didn't mean Sabrina herself was on the up-and-up, but he doubted someone who *was* on the side of right would be out there shooting at him and her, no matter how bad *she* might be.

She'd trusted her instincts to push him down and avoid the gunshot. Well, he had his own instincts, even if they'd apparently dulled a bit when it came to finding himself the potential target of a gunman.

"I can't let you—I couldn't let anyone—go out in this alone. It isn't smart, feasible, and like I said before, would probably end up in me being called to rescue you anyway. I'll stick it out. Froggy will help track the guy down."

"It's dangerous. Life and death of the shooting kind, not the buried alive kind."

"I got that."

She nodded, serious and focused. "If your SAR friends send reinforcements, it puts them in harm's way."

Connor cataloged all the people he worked with. He wasn't the only one with military experience, but he definitely had the most recent experience. His team was tough, focused and dedicated.

But there wasn't even one of them he'd want to risk. Too many had families, responsibilities, lives outside this little mountain range that had become Connor's entire world.

"I'll call them off," he said gruffly. Her raised eyebrows were the only sign she was surprised by his assessment. "But I don't think we should go into this unarmed."

"I'm not."

"You keep saying that—"

She patted her coat at her chest. "One holstered here." Then she pointed to her pack. "An arsenal in there."

"A bit heavy."

"I do just fine." She paused to consider something, then shrugged her pack off. She rifled around, then pulled out a secured Glock. "You know how to use one of these?"

"Yeah."

"This ain't a navy rifle."

He tried not to let her purposeful barbs land, but she sure knew how to aim them. "I can shoot a Glock. Want a demonstration?"

"Maybe later when I've got time to get all hot and bothered. Got anything to carry it with?"

"No," he muttered irritably.

"I think I've got a back holster in here." She dug some more in her pack.

"You can't really think you're going to hike around a mountain with all that weight on your back."

"Why not?" She pulled out a holster that would indeed fit onto the back of his pants. Not really where he wanted a gun, but it'd have to do.

"In this weather, in the distance we might need to go, you want the lightest pack possible."

"Sure, but I'm not hiking for fun. I'm hiking to take down a guy before he kills anyone. I'll have my arsenal with me, thanks."

"Speed should be a consideration."

"It will be. But the weight of the pack's not holding me back yet. Want to bet how long it will take me before it does?"

He looked her up and down, and realized before he'd finished the sweep this woman would always be too contrary to admit she was wrong if there was a bet. "No."

She grinned. "Good. Now, you got any safe ways we can follow him without walking through this big open get-yourself-shot-in-the-head clearing here?"

Since he could see that eventuality just a little too clearly in his head, Connor sighed. "You have such a way with words."

SABRINA CHUCKLED. SHE wasn't sure about the guy's skills, but at least he wasn't too much of a bore to be around.

"It'll take longer to take the safe route. You have enough prepared in that backpack of horrors if we have to be out here through the night?" he asked.

She had no doubt the Boy Scout here was. Beyond that, she'd prepared for everything she could. Anything to bring this guy in. "Yup."

"All right. If we move east here, we can wrap around the mountain with some decent cover." He pointed at the direction he wanted to go, looking big and authoritative in black and orange in the midst of all this white. "They'll be some clearings to cross, but unless he follows our path, we should be okay."

Sabrina nodded. She maneuvered from lying on her stomach into a low crouch. The top of her head would likely be visible from wherever the hit man had been, but as no shots rang out, she had to believe he'd run off.

She wasn't the target after all, and there'd be no reason for Connor to be one. Oh, a hit man hired by this kind of shady black market group would no doubt kill them both if they were in the way, but she and Connor weren't the *target*.

She'd hold onto that. It was a shame she didn't have snow camo to see her through this part. "I'll get up first. If there's no shooting, you come up behind."

"You may have been right about the whole someone's about to shoot us thing, but hiking this mountain is *my* expertise. You're going to let me lead."

Sabrina had to bite back her initial, knee-jerk response to that. The fact she *could* meant her tactical training had finally taken over. Instead of sniping with him, she considered. And realized he was right, no matter how irritated she was by it. Or the heavy-handed way he was trying to *order* her. It had been a long time since Sabrina had taken orders from someone she didn't fully trust and respect.

But desperate times called for desperate, self-controlling measures. "All right. You lead us to the rock face over there. Then what?"

"We'll use Froggy to track. Probably going to be edging toward nightfall anyway, so even if there were *actual* tracks, we won't be able to see them."

"You need to call off your team."

He'd agreed to do it, but there was a hesitation in him now. She had the sense he was doing the same thing she'd just done—fighting off knee-jerk arguments in favor of considering what was best for their situation.

He lifted the comm unit attached to his coat to his mouth. "Iona. Copy?"

"Copy."

"I'm calling off the search. All signs point to this guy getting off the mountain on his own. But you saw him, right? You could describe him?"

"Well, sure."

"Give a description to the local police, and let them know he escaped rescue, and therefore might be dangerous."

There was a long pause of static as Sabrina had to fight with the rising need to rip the comm unit out of his hand and demand to know what the hell he thought he was doing. Getting cops involved was a terrible idea.

"Dangerous?" the woman's voice said carefully.

"It's possible. And they should know," Connor said, but as he spoke the words he maintained eye contact with Sabrina.

She wanted to punch him.

"Are you sure about this, Connor. What about the wom—"

"I'm sure. I'm headed back to the cabin. Do not send out another team. Understood?"

"Connor—"

"Understood?" Connor repeated, and Sabrina could all but see him in tactical gear barking orders at a navy SEAL team. She hadn't been needling him when she'd said he looked too young to be a retired SEAL and she had to wonder what kind of injury could have taken him out of commission. Much like her, he'd clearly recovered from it.

"All right. If you're sure."

"Get the description to the police, then forget about it. Over and out." He didn't reattach the unit to his coat. He took the whole thing off, and turned a switch Sabrina had to assume shut the unit off completely.

He shoved it into his pack. Cutting ties. That was good for what she was trying to do, but she had to wonder. "You sure she'll listen?"

"Mostly. This lasts too long she's going to send a group after me, but I imagine she'll wait a few days."

"Why'd you involve the cops?" Sabrina tried to keep the scathing note out of her tone. She could be equitable for the sake of teamwork. "Basically signing them a death warrant," she added. Okay, maybe not *equitable*.

"No, I'm covering my bases," Connor replied. "If he gets off the mountain without us knowing about it, they'll have a heads-up. And so will we."

Sabrina shook her head. For a former SEAL this guy really seemed to underestimate how dangerous the bad guy could be.

"You ready?" he demanded.

"Ready."

Even though he was leading them, she still stood first, gun cocked and ready.

He stared at the gun. "Where'd you… How'd you get that out without me seeing?" he asked, eyebrows drawn together.

It lifted her spirits some. She smirked. "Magic, baby."

Chapter Six

No shots rang out when Connor stood up alongside Sabrina. So, he led her and Froggy on the path that would give them the most cover. They walked in silence except for the crunching of their feet on the snow. Even that was muted.

They both knew how to move through a landscape with stealth and care. To be aware of their surroundings. But the gunman seemed to have run or hunkered down, because there were no more sightings, and no more gut feelings from Sabrina having them hit the deck before shots rang out.

The quiet and the hike gave Connor time to think. Really think. In a way he hadn't been able to since he'd gotten the rescue call this morning. The way he preferred to. A lining up of facts and thoughts that would clarify some things for him. Because even though he'd agreed to help Sabrina, there was this nagging feeling he needed to know *what* she was, not just who.

The fake cop thing she had pulled at the rescue site wouldn't be out of character for some kind of bounty hunter, and a military background would be beneficial in that kind of work. Though bounty hunters could skirt the law a little bit, they were usually bringing in someone who should be brought in. It fit.

But it didn't.

What he knew about Brina Killian from Nate, was that she was—or had been—a woman with superior drive who'd blow up her life after her SEAL goals had been ended by a freak injury. In Nate's estimation, Sabrina was an all-or-nothing type. Bounty hunters lived in a gray area that didn't quite work with that personality.

Granted, Nate could have been wrong about Sabrina. He'd been wrong about other things, which was half of why Connor was here and not a SEAL. Still, while Nate blamed himself for everything that had gone wrong, Connor didn't. He'd had free will. He'd trusted Nate's assessment of a dangerous situation.

They'd both been wrong. They'd both paid the price.

That was way beside the point of what he was trying to figure out now. Sabrina Killian was his focus, and he didn't think she was a bounty hunter.

The situation itself screamed mercenary to him. And yet, that didn't ring true. There was something about her—no matter how brash, no matter how happy to lie about the cop thing or irritate him on purpose— that he couldn't equate with mercenary. She had a sense of fairness about her. An ease at working with him, even when she didn't fully want to be.

Maybe the facts added up, but his instincts told him *false*.

In search and rescue, fact was more important

than instinct. And yet, instinct always played a role in decision-making. When it came to people, Connor had always found it imperative.

But when instinct warred with fact, especially when he had time to think, a lot of past failures undercut the clear truth, or the right way forward.

Did it matter what she was? When they'd been shot at? So clearly whoever she was hunting was equally as bad as whatever she was up to. When every time he had the chance to decide to let her go off alone, to let this be out of his hands, he refused?

"Tell me why I should think you're anything but a mercenary," he said as they weaved through a thicket of whitebark pine.

"I never said I wasn't."

Which clarified the argument he'd been having with himself. "But you're not." He might not know this woman, but based on the way she'd acted, what he could glean from having been friends with her ex-boyfriend once upon a time, that wasn't the way she operated.

Mostly because if she *was* a mercenary, she wouldn't let him think she was.

She didn't say anything else. Didn't argue with him or explain. She just kept hiking. He snuck a look over his shoulder at her, wondering if the weight of her pack was getting to her. But she followed him with easy strides, not breathing too heavily even as they went up in elevation. She looked calm and collected and at ease. The only sign this wasn't a leisurely walk on a nice day was the fact the very tip of her nose was red.

They came to a series of boulders. Connor eyed them, thought about the terrain he knew like the back of his hand. He brought up a mental map of the area in his mind. They'd have to climb this series of rocks to give them cover to get to the main cliff face they were headed for.

He started to climb, thinking about what might get through to her. No matter what he'd told her, or anyone else, he didn't know what it was like for an injury to ruin his military career. Still, his had ended abruptly and because of a mistake, so he knew what happened in the aftermath of sudden loss. Whatever she was doing here, whoever had sent her, this *had* to connect to the end of her military career.

"Leaving the military is rough," he said, trying to strike a conversational tone. "Finding something to do with those skills is a really lucky thing." He climbed over the next rock easily enough, holding Froggy's leash and watching her with an eagle eye to make sure the dog wasn't overtaxing herself.

Sabrina snorted behind him. She eyed the rock between them. "Luck doesn't have a thing to do with where I am."

"Then what do you call it?" He considered her standing below him. "Sheer force of will to build your life into something different than you planned, but equally fulfilling?" Because the way this job meant so much to her that she wouldn't give up spoke to it being some kind of satisfaction for her.

She frowned up at him for a moment. He couldn't possibly read what was going on in that brain of hers.

"Some of it's will, sure," she said, climbing up the first rock between them. She shrugged as if will was nothing.

Definitely not what he would have expected.

She scrabbled up a rock taller than her. When she got the top, she looked down at him from her crouched position. "Don't you believe in destiny?"

She went from crouching to standing at her full height at the top of a rock, the sun haloing her body in gold. Loose tendrils of dark hair danced around her face and her expression was fierce and goddess-like.

Something heavy and irrevocable seemed to flip over in his chest. "Hell no," he said, but his voice came out rusty.

She hopped down so they were on the even ground again. That odd moment gone, thank *God*. Though he wouldn't mind her not being so close.

"I do. Sheer force of will. Luck." She waved them both off. "If I believed in those I'd have given up on life the minute my hip shattered. And I tried. Boy did I. But some things are *meant*, Connor. Destiny is where you're meant to be, knowing who you're meant to know, doing what you're supposed to do."

"With no choice?" he asked blandly. She was trying to pull one over on him, surely.

"There's always a choice. It's all we've got on this crazy ride around the sun. But destiny is where you end up when you make all the right choices." She tilted her head, studied him from below and managed to make it seem like she was a queen inspecting a commoner.

"Do you really think you survived the military, got into SAR, because of *luck*?"

She sounded so dismissive he had to fight the need to bristle. The need to argue with her. What did her opinion matter? He hadn't meant everything was about luck anyway. And what was the difference between luck and "destiny" anyway?

"Well?" she asked, pointing to the route ahead. "What's the holdup?"

She wanted him to keep walking, keep leading her to the hit man. And he should. That's absolutely what he should do. But he found himself studying her, trying to puzzle her out first.

"I'm not going to tell you what I am, Connor. Why I am. And if that bothers you, you're free to vamoose."

Vamoose.

"I'm not going anywhere, *Brina.*"

She had a knife in her hand, pointed at him, and he had *no* idea where it had come from or how she'd gotten it there. She could move, that was for sure. He supposed he should feel more fear than admiration but he couldn't quite work past awe.

"I want to make something very clear," she said, her voice as sharp as the blade she held. "You don't call me that. It's not my name. That's a past I left behind and nobody, and I mean *nobody*, gets to remind me of it. We clear?"

HE DIDN'T APPEAR to be worried, threatened or even scared at the fact she'd only need one good jab to take a piece out of him. Which poked at Sabrina's temper even more.

"Clear," he eventually said.

She should have been gratified he'd stand down. Happy he understood she was *dangerous* if she wanted to be.

But she felt small and foolish and *pissed.* Because she'd given too much of herself away. He'd pushed a button and she'd allowed herself to explode, rather than play it cool and win the game in the end.

Exhaustion tried to sneak over her. She'd been working hard following this guy and she finally had this lead, but in the midst of all this cold, and the heavy weight of her pack, she wanted to curl up and sleep.

Which wasn't an option. Nor was getting all worked up that he'd used her old nickname. She'd give herself a break at the overreaction. What did it matter in the short run? They were working together. Better he know her sore spots and avoid them.

If he tried to poke at them, she'd just leave him in the dust. She eyed the dog. Maybe even take Froggy with her. The dog was on a leash, and Sabrina knew a few dog commands. All she'd have to do was snatch it and run. Oh, the guy would fight for his dog, but Sabrina might be able to win the fight.

She shook her head. Bad habit, always trying to find ways to escape the situation she was in. Ditch the partners she was supposed to be working with. If there was anything North Star had taught her, it was that teamwork could be invaluable. She couldn't dismiss it out of hand just because the other person was a jerk. Especially if they were a skilled, knowledgeable jerk.

Unfortunately, Connor fit the bill.

"What's your last name?" she demanded, searching for equilibrium and a place her past wouldn't haunt her. All these years at North Star she'd been able to leave Brina behind. Why was that iteration of herself back to haunt her now? Why did she *care*?

"Why do you want to know my last name?" Connor asked, easily climbing another boulder and jumping to the next.

"You know mine. Why shouldn't I know yours?" She followed him, knowing her leaps weren't as graceful, but they got the job done. *Story of your life, Sabrina.*

"Because I don't know what your business is or who you'll pass my last name along to."

"It'd be easy enough to find out your name whether you tell me or not."

"Probably."

"So why don't you just tell me?"

"I'd rather you have to do the work. Which you won't be able to do while we're out here."

"That's what you think," she muttered. Thanks to Elsie's IT expertise, Sabrina's North Star phone could do a whole heck of a lot.

But she didn't tell him that. She followed him. Through the cold and the white. It would have been pretty and exhilarating if they weren't following and on the lookout for an assassin. She'd always loved the mountains. A sharp contrast to the Kansas flat she'd grown up in.

She'd always thought she could have enjoyed that flat, felt at home there. But her father's strict rules and expectations had made her feel as beat down as that hardscrabble patch of land he'd tried to use her as a tool to farm.

The navy had been her escape. She'd run away, joined up and found a purpose that had finally, *finally* felt like freedom. The rigidness, the orders, she'd understood all that thanks to dear old Dad. But getting to go places, set her own goals and strive toward them had been all the freedom she'd ever wanted.

Her throat felt tight and her eyes burned. The altitude getting to her, surely. Either way, if she wasn't going to think about her life as Brina, she really wasn't going to think about her father.

She felt her phone vibrate in her pocket. She considered Connor's easy gait. She'd struggle to keep up with him if she surreptitiously stopped. She'd likely fall and break her neck if she tried to jump boulders and talk on her phone.

"Hold up, Connor," she said, imbuing the casual statement with enough bite to sound like an order. Just the way she hoped would irritate him. She brought the phone to her ear.

"You're not going to have serv—"

"Shay? What's up?"

Connor's voice was obnoxiously loud next to her so that Sabrina didn't quite pick up on Shay's words.

"I don't believe you've actually got anyone on the line," he said irritably. "You're just trying to—"

"Do you *mind*?" she retorted. She hit speaker, and Shay's voice echoed in the space between them. She smirked, clicked speaker off, then turned away from Connor. "Must have lost you for a second, can you repeat that?"

"I just needed to give you an update on some things. First, we've got Holden. He's got a lead, and it's taking a team of us to work through it. I've had to pull some of the team I had closer to you as backup. I'm going to have to call in some outside help to send your way if—"

"I don't need any backup. I got this."

"Sabrina." There was censure in Shay's tone, but Sabrina didn't need it.

"Seriously. I've got this SAR guy working with me. Former navy SEAL. He wants to track down the guy as much as I do. But until we do, and even once we do, it's two against one. Holden may need a team. I don't."

"It's not a competition."

No, it wasn't. It was Holden's life. "I'm good, Shay. I promise."

There was a pause. A sigh. "I'm glad you've got someone with skills helping you, but we're talking about a hit man."

"We're talking about me," Sabrina replied, trying to sound her brash and cocky self even as relief Holden was okay made her feel a bit too soft. "Look, you want to pull some outside help and station them close as an emergency to make yourself feel better, that's fine. But you know I'm not going to call on strangers. Take care of Holden's lead first. Mine's pretty straightforward."

"Do you remember that I'm in charge here?"

Sabrina laughed. "Yeah, I also remember some things you did when Granger was in charge that weren't exactly 'sir, yes, sir.'"

It was Shay's turn to chuckle. "Yeah, that feels like a lifetime ago. Listen. I'm putting some people on standby. When I think I can spare Gabe or Mallory, I'm sending them your way. If you need help, it'll be close. I know you'll avoid it at all costs, but I also know you're smart enough, and care about getting this guy enough, that you'll call in backup if you need it."

"Low blow," Sabrina muttered.

"That's why I'm the boss. Watch your back, Sab. This might be a little bit more complicated than we were planning on it being."

Sabrina eyed the angry mountain man former SEAL staring at her with blue eyes the color of spring skies. Yeah, *complicated* was no joke.

Chapter Seven

She ended the call. He'd gleaned she was talking to her boss or some kind of leader. Though clearly Sabrina could make a lot of her own choices when it came to how to proceed.

He was slightly surprised that Sabrina had told the person she'd talked to about him. That she hadn't tried to pretend she was handling this alone, or that her boss hadn't demanded more information about who he was.

Mercenary seemed less and less possible.

"How do you get service up here?" he asked. That was another odd piece to the puzzle.

She fluttered her lashes. "Magic."

He'd figured she wouldn't tell him, but it had been worth a shot. "Yeah, you keep saying that. So strange how I don't buy it. You're not some secret government group, are you?"

"Why, Con, you got something against Uncle Sam?"

Boy, did he. But he wasn't about to air that here, or with her. Still, if she had moved into some government group... Distaste moved through him. He would have preferred working with a mercenary.

"You *do* have something against Uncle Sam," Sabrina said, seeming delighted with the idea.

"Didn't say that."

"Didn't have to. Your sneer says it all."

"I am *not* sneering. Even if I was, you're walking behind me and can't see my face."

"But I can see your posture. That's a sneering posture."

"You're one strange lady, you know that?"

"Been told that a time or two. Doesn't bother me much. Usually all strange means is different than so-and-so, and who wants to be so-and-so?"

"We're going to have to find a place to camp soon."

"Don't you think we should hike through the night?"

"Not unless you want to break a leg. Either in the dark or tomorrow when you're dizzy from lack of sleep."

"For a former SEAL, you're kind of a baby."

Connor did not huff out an irritated breath though he wanted to. He wasn't going to be needled into forgoing safety precautions. "We break for dark. Nonnegotiable."

"You don't seem to understand this guy is a hit man. Meaning he has a target he's trying to kill. It's life or death we stop him before he does kill."

"Who exactly is this man after in the middle of the Tetons? What innocent bystander is going to get offed in the middle of the night with a storm threatening?" Connor spread his arms out. "No one is out here but the three of us. On a good day—" This time he pointed at the sky. "If you haven't noticed, it's not a good day. So who would he be after?"

"I don't…" She bit off the remainder of the sentence, but he could tell by her frustration exactly what she'd been about to say.

"You don't know. You don't know who his target is." Great. Just *great*. She probably *was* with the government with this level of ineptitude.

"Not exactly. And it isn't my job to know. It's just my job to stop him. We spend the night, he puts more miles between us. He reaches that target, kills him and disappears. You don't know how hard it was to track him down in the first place."

He turned to face her, to stop their forward progress. "What do you know about this guy?"

"What I need to," she retorted.

But he didn't think so. "You don't know *anything* about this guy." Not a question. Clearly, she was acting in the dark.

"I know he's the guy I'm after. That's all I need to know."

"CIA? Some stupid offshoot where the minute you screw up you're out on your butt? I'd say FBI, but that mouth of yours wouldn't last a day."

She raised her eyebrows, let out a low whistle. "Man, what exactly happened when you left the SEALs? They mess you up? Didn't give you the sendoff you'd come to think you deserved?"

"Keep trying." She'd never guess, and he had to be careful to guard his temper so it didn't come spilling out, all pointless vitriol that didn't change a damn thing.

Nothing she was involved in changed what had happened, and it certainly didn't help that she was connected, no matter how much ancient history, to Nate Averly.

Which was all over and done and not what mattered in the here and now. He jabbed a finger in her direction. "You need me. You can't track him out here on your own. Not when a storm's about to unleash. So, pretend like you're going to run off. Two things will happen— you either come crawling back, or you freeze to death."

"Actually, there's a third option." She nodded meaningfully at Froggy.

Connor's hands tightened on the leash and he couldn't hold back a sneer. "You try to touch my dog, I won't be responsible for what I do in return."

She rolled her eyes. "Take it easy, hotshot. You got responsible etched into the fiber of your being."

He wanted to shout. To fight. He *wanted* to turn back the clock and make a whole bunch of different decisions. Ones that kept this woman far, *far* away from him.

But he couldn't do that, and shouting and fighting was a waste of energy when they were facing tough roads ahead.

Someone had to be even-tempered. *Someone* had to do the right thing. And that someone was him. Beginning and end of story. *Always*.

"He's either going to have to find shelter himself, or he's going to die of the elements. I know this mountain. I know those clouds. Unless his target is within a five-mile radius of him, he can't get to anyone before this storm hits. That I can guarantee you."

For the first time Sabrina didn't retort right away. She looked up at the sky, kept quiet and seemed to really *consider*.

"Guarantee, huh?" She studied him skeptically.

He nodded. "If he knows what he's doing, and based on what we've seen, I think he does. He knew how to fake an injury by rappelling down a cliff. He knew how to take off and disappear when you were about to get to him. He's not out here by accident. He's out here by design. So, let's take the leap he knows what he's doing. He's going to camp. It's what I'd do. Even if my target was close. Because no matter how close the target, if you can't finish them off, there's no point risking giving yourself away."

"He gave himself away when he shot at us."

"Only because we were already after him. What if the target doesn't know he's a target?"

"I don't think they do."

Connor nodded. "Then he's got time. Or thinks he does. We're a wrinkle, but again, storm's coming. Maybe he'll assume we're not as smart as him. Maybe he won't. But you don't survive, you can't kill the people and get the payoff. Right?"

She scowled, not answering the question, which he knew meant he'd scored a point.

"And if *you* don't survive, you can't stop the guy." He tapped his temple. "So, use your head."

"I'd like to use your head as a battering ram," she

muttered, clearly because she couldn't out-reason him. Not when he was right.

But all that scowling and irritation melted off her face and she smiled brightly up at him. "You got a tent built for two in that big pack of yours?"

Hell.

SABRINA KNEW SHE'D scored a point when Connor's superior expression went a little lax. Because naturally he'd have a tent, but one of those flimsy backpacking deals meant to be light and certainly not built to shelter two people.

Especially when one of the people was as tall and broad as he was.

But he recovered, quickly enough. "We'll need a lookout anyway, just in case your friend decides to take some interest in us. We'll take turns. Froggy will rest when I do."

"Don't trust me with your dog?"

"Lady, I don't trust you with my *hat*."

She smirked, because it wasn't precisely true. He was trusting her with some things or he wouldn't be here. Still, the wind was screaming and her pack was damn heavy. There hadn't been any snow or other precipitation yet, but Sabrina figured it was a matter of time.

She'd survived just as bad, if not worse, and sometimes alone. Bad weather, cold weather didn't scare her. Didn't mean she was going to enjoy herself overnight.

"We need to find a good place to camp. Some shelter from the wind. Some cover from the hit man wandering about."

"Not wandering. Whatever he's doing. He's got a plan." That she was sure of now. "Unless he had a gun on him when you lifted him up?"

"He didn't," Connor said gravely, ducking his head against the wind as he headed forward toward another cluster of boulders. "Could have had a knife or something on him, but no gun. I would have felt it when I boarded him."

Sabrina nodded though she knew he couldn't see her. Still, it proved her point. "He had a gun hidden up here. Did he have something on him that could have been ammo?"

Connor's stride didn't hitch, but she sensed him go back over the course of events. "He had stuff in his pockets. I didn't pat him down."

"So, he could have had the ammo he picked up— which is how I tracked him. Gun hidden somewhere up here on the mountain."

Connor stopped and turned to look at her. He had to raise his voice against the howling wind. "Why the fake rescue then?"

That was the question.

He shook his head and went back to hiking. "You don't know either."

"No. I don't. But it's something we should think about. He didn't have a gun. Then he had one."

"I still maintain it could be two different guys."

"But you know it's not."

When he didn't respond to that, she figured it was as good as assent. But *why the fake rescue* was something she hadn't had time to fully turn over in her mind yet. "What if the target is someone in SAR?"

This time Connor came to an abrupt halt. Then he shook his head. "Why the hell would you say that?"

"Because the only way the fake rescue makes sense—having that kind of contact with people in an uncontrolled situation without a gun—is to see how someone would be rescued or who would be doing the rescuing. Don't know why a hit man would care about the first. We both know why a hit man would care about the second."

Connor started walking again. He said nothing, didn't even grunt. Sabrina had to assume that meant he was thinking about it. So, Sabrina continued to roll it over in her mind.

"You got any cops or the like in your group? That seems the most obvious option. Someone in law enforcement. Someone who could have ticked off some criminals."

"No one who's in current law enforcement. Possibly someone has it in their history. I'm not in charge of hiring, so unless someone mentioned it, I wouldn't know."

"Could you find out?"

"I'd have to use that fancy phone of yours."

Sabrina considered it. "No, we don't want to raise any red flags." Elsie might be able to look into it, if she wasn't caught up in Holden's mission. Sabrina would send her a text later.

"Here," Connor said. "We'll camp here."

She didn't care for the *order*, like he was in charge

of her or something. She surveyed the area. Flat. Sort of. Surrounded on most sides by boulders. It would certainly protect them from the wind. She turned in a slow circle looking at higher ground. She didn't see any good places that someone would be able to get a shot off from. Granted, those peaks and cliffs could be concealing places to hide or shoot from, but she didn't think they were going to get a better spot.

"You really think stopping is our best course of action?" Normally she would have flat-out argued with him about it, but he was the expert when it came to this stuff, and he'd brought up some good points earlier. She was torn. Not certain.

Something she really hated.

"It's the *only* course of action."

Sabrina rolled her eyes, but she didn't argue with him. Dark was encroaching. God, she was cold. And tired. And *hungry*. Taking care of her basic needs would allow her to complete her mission without making a critical mistake.

Didn't mean stopping and waiting suited her any.

Before Connor did anything he pulled some contraption out of his pack, which turned out to be a foldable water and food bowl for the dog. He filled both, and Froggy eagerly ate and drank to her heart's content.

Only then did Connor set about securing them some shelter. He set a little tarp down then put his backpack on it and began to spread out supplies.

"What can I do?"

He looked up at her as if surprised she could be helpful. Cooperative. And, okay, his surprise was probably warranted. Working with a partner didn't come naturally to her, especially one whose skills outmatched hers in this one small particular area.

Still. She could do what she had to do to survive. Even be helpful and ask questions.

"I'll get the tent set up. You can handle food. I've got an MRE in each of our packs. Probably be good for us both to do the heating up rather than eat them cold."

"An MRE. I haven't had one of those in eons. I didn't miss them." The ready-to-eat meals that had been part of her military career did not inspire excitement for the meal ahead.

"They'll keep you full."

"I know what they'll do," Sabrina muttered. She pulled out the tarp Connor had made her pack back at his cabin. She spread it out to keep herself from having to kneel or sit in the snow.

She got out the MRE pouches from her pack and then Connor's and followed the instructions to utilize the flameless heater to warm the food while Connor built up the flimsy-looking tent.

"That thing going to hold in all this wind?"

He stepped back and studied his work. "That's why we camped here. Won't keep us out of the wind completely, but the boulders should block the worst of it. Sleeping in shifts won't just be to keep a watch for our hit man, it'll be imperative to make sure the winds don't damage the tent."

She handed him the warm part of his MRE and he

took a seat next to her on the spread-out tarp, though kept enough space between them to almost be laughable. Sabrina was about to make a joke about sharing body heat, but Froggy curled up in between them, which turned out to be a nice warmth.

Darkness was encroaching, spreading across the world around them. The stars winked to life, bright beacons of peace. Sabrina didn't care much for peace or stillness. Much as she'd love to appreciate the beauty of a night sky spread out before her without being dimmed by city lights or human interference, the quiet and the stillness required often led to reflection.

Sabrina tried to avoid reflection at all costs. It made her think about her father, and how even though she'd cut off all ties, even though he'd been a terrible dad, she'd mourned when she'd heard he'd died.

It made her think about how she'd put everything she was into becoming a navy SEAL. So sure it would be the thing that magically made her feel *right* in her own skin. In this world.

It made her think about the pain of her injury. Which made her think about Nate. And how the man next to her knew and had been a SEAL side by side with Nate. What were the chances?

The world was small because whatever higher power was up there sure liked messing with people.

"Does search and rescue make up for it?" she found herself asking, when she knew she shouldn't. But star shine was as good as a couple whiskey shooters in her world. Loosened her tongue and her inhibitions. Made her feel big and bright and too aware of the loneliness inside of her she'd been burying since her mother had died when she'd been five.

"Make up for what?" Connor asked roughly.

"You know what."

He heaved out a sigh. She couldn't see him in the dark. He was just a faint shadow in the silvery light of stars and moon. But she sensed…a similar restlessness inside of him.

Or you're cold and tired enough to be delirious.

"Doing SAR… At first, it helped. Suddenly not being able to *do* anything was hard, so search and rescue felt like doing. Now, I think it's better than anything I could have done as a SEAL."

"You're saving dummies who didn't follow directions."

Connor snorted out a laugh. "Sometimes, sure, but those dummies are just people who overestimated their own abilities. Haven't we all been there?"

"You're nicer than I am, Con."

"No doubt."

And she'd blame it on the stars that it made her feel a little mushy toward him. Though he took care of that pretty quick as the stars shone and the wind howled and the first flakes of snow began to fall.

"I think I know who the target could be," Connor said quietly. So quietly she almost convinced herself he hadn't spoken at all.

"Oh yeah? Someone on SAR, yeah? You should probably contact them. Forewarned and all that."

"Right."

Sabrina dug her phone out of her pocket. "Here."

He shook his head. "Don't need it."

When she only stared at him in confusion, he huffed out a breath.

"Buy a clue, Sabrina."

Chapter Eight

"You?" Sabrina demanded. "Why you?"

Connor rubbed a gloved hand over his face. Both were cold. Because of the weather. Because ever since she'd said the target could be someone on his team he'd known...

"Law enforcement aren't the only people who make enemies." Not that he'd understood he *had* enemies, but it made sense. More sense than Iona being some kind of target.

"Explain."

It was an order, and he didn't have to obey any orders from this woman, but it seemed they both had information the other needed. She knew something more about this hit man than she'd let on, and he knew...

Nate had warned him, hadn't he? That they were in danger. That getting rid of them hadn't been enough for whoever was pulling the strings.

Connor had listened to his friend and convinced himself Nate had paranoia born of PTSD. But this fit every single thing Nate had said that Connor had brushed off as the ravings of someone who needed professional help.

It made his stomach twist and turn, but he'd been warned that he could be a target. He just hadn't listened. "And if it's connected to me, it's connected to Nate. He'd be a target too."

"What?" Sabrina demanded. She got to her feet and began to pace. "Explain this."

"I'm not sure I know how." His own mind reeled with possibilities, and had since he'd begun to work through the options. It didn't *quite* make sense, but it made more sense than anything else.

"Try," she gritted out through clenched teeth.

He noted she was *working* to keep a lid on her temper, which he knew meant this was important. But the truth was words escaped him. There was only feeling and instinct.

He could be wrong. God, he hoped he was wrong, but this was the kind of thing he'd always been waiting for. Not a hit man. Not the *danger* Nate had always been going on and on about, so much Connor had pulled away, called him less and less, answered his calls less and less. Until they were barely friends.

But he'd always been subconsciously waiting for something from that confusing time to pop up and finally make sense.

"I'm not sure I can work out exactly *why* I'd be a target, but if I line up all the evidence, I'm the only one who fits. The truth is, I've always wondered, waited for…something. Not a hit out on me, but *something*.

Because the way Nate and I were not so honorably discharged has never set quite right with me."

She stopped pacing and just stared at him, even though she couldn't have seen the expression on his face in the dark any more than he could see hers. "You said you were injured. That's why—"

"I lied," Connor sad flatly. "I've had to lie. I was *told* to lie." Which was why he hadn't gone home like Nate had. Lies didn't come easily to Connor, so he'd had to carve out a new, isolated life away from his family and the people he'd want to tell the truth to.

"That doesn't make any sense."

"No, it didn't. It doesn't," Connor agreed. He was doing his level best to remain calm, to reason this out, and weirdly Sabrina...helped. She was all edges and angles and he felt the need to be calm and smooth in response.

"Start at the beginning. If you weren't injured, why were you discharged?"

"Nate and I were part of an operation. A lot of groundwork in this village. Nate thought he had an in with a civilian. He—*we*—trusted the wrong guy. We learned this resulted in a major intel breach. We were blamed, ousted, then told to pretend it was an injury that ended our SEAL careers."

"That doesn't make any sense. Doesn't the military love a scapegoat?"

"Yeah, they do. That's why it never set right. Why not just...blame us and be done with it? Sure, you'd have to do the trial thing, but if it was true—wouldn't they win the trial? Why did we have to pretend? It always felt…wrong. Like we'd stumbled into something bigger than what we were doing. Or knew we were doing."

Sabrina was quiet for a while, and Connor felt the need to…fill in the silence. He didn't want to tell her about Nate, about how little he'd believed him. Not so much because it hurt his pride to be wrong, but because she could very well have the same opinion he'd held for so long.

"Nate's always said there was more to it, and to watch my back. The more I settled into my life here, the less I believed him. But the guy coming when *I'd* rescue him? When no one else was out that far on the trail? It adds up." *Hell.* It added up. Nate had been right. Not paranoid. *Right.*

"Couldn't someone else in your SAR group have some secret they're hiding? I'm not discounting your story, I just don't understand… What I know doesn't make sense with the military."

Connor let himself consider, beyond his own personal feelings and instincts. "Possible, but not probable. If this hit man or whoever did their homework enough to know who they'd have rescue them, the group is small. Iona is our only helicopter pilot—and the location was pretty much only reachable quickly by helicopter. She doesn't have anything in her background. I'd know."

There was a slight, tense pause. "Would you?"

"Yeah, I would." Uncomfortable with her implication, God knew why, Connor rubbed a gloved hand over Froggy's head. "We've been working together since I started. She's got a husband and three kids. We spend a lot of time together." Frustrated he felt the need to defend himself, he grumbled the rest. "I'm her youngest kid's godfather, for Pete's sake. I'd know if she had something going on."

"Would she know the same about you?"

Connor considered. "She wouldn't know what, but I'd bet a lot of money if someone asked her if I had something lurking in my past, she'd say yes."

"There's no one else who would have been called out to rescue?"

"Today? No. I was on call for this precise sort of thing through the end of the week. We don't exactly publicize our schedule, but it wouldn't be hard to find out either. I'm the only full-time guy on our crew."

"So you really make the most sense, even aside from your macho pride."

She said it so glibly, it poked at his temper. "My... You're a real piece of work, Sabrina."

"Yeah, don't forget it. So, you get blamed for an intel breach. You and Nate. No one else in your team?"

"No. We were the only ones involved in communicating with this civilian."

"You know anything about the civilian?"

"Aside from the fact he's likely a terrorist, and the name he gave us was fake, no."

"You're blamed for this breach. Dishonorable discharge, but they tell you to fake an injury."

Connor debated the rest of it. He wasn't sure she needed the truth about Nate when this was about him. Except if it *was* about him, it'd be about Nate too. Nate might be a target too. He might not know who Sabrina worked for, but stopping this hit man was more important than pretty much anything at this point.

"I was told to fake an injury. Nate didn't have to."

"What?" Sabrina said, a breathlessness like she'd been delivered a blow. Maybe she still had feelings for Nate. That certainly shouldn't *bother* Connor. And didn't. At all.

"The informant, or supposed informant, had shot him. I was discharged and sent back to the States before Nate was. He had to recover. They told me not to contact him, so I assume they told him the same."

"But you did."

"Of course I did. He went home to Montana and…" Connor wasn't comfortable with the level of subterfuge he'd used to contact Nate. It had been for the sake of Nate's paranoia, but Connor had done it. Now, it seemed he'd actually made the right choice. "I made sure no one would be able to find out I did, but we got in touch. We both knew it was fishy, but neither of us knew what to do about it." Nate had wanted to press. To investigate secretly. To wage their own war. Connor had suggested gently he see the therapist at the rehabilitation facility he was at.

He couldn't feel guilty about that now. There was no time for it. But he also didn't need to let Sabrina in on the specifics. "We agreed to let it go. Get on with our lives."

Sabrina laughed. Which was so incongruous to the situation, Nate could only stare at her shadow in the dark. "Why are you *laughing*?"

"I mean, maybe Nate had a personality transplant, but if he didn't, there's no way that stubborn mule let *anything* go."

Connor sighed. Then just rested his head in his hands. "No, he didn't let it go. I just didn't believe him."

SABRINA FELT SOME sympathy for Connor. The resignation in his voice was guilt and blame, heaped only on himself. But she didn't have time to try and deal with the feeling. "So, Nate keeps digging. Whatever and whoever was hiding something, well, they'd have a reason to silence you two, wouldn't they?"

"I… I guess. I don't know. Silence us? We don't know anything."

"They sure think you do." Whoever *they* were. And how did it connect to the military? "Jeez, this is a cluster. But I need to share it with my group."

"You're with the government."

He said it so flatly, so devoid of any and all emotion it was almost comical. Especially since he was wrong. She could have let him think it. Part of her thought she should, just to prove she didn't have a soft spot. But she *did* have one. Sadly for her, an epically big one for do-gooders. "No, you're safe there."

"So, what then?" he asked suspiciously. "Not a cop. Not the government."

"I work for a private group. With private interests— ones that work for the good guys. Only and always."

"Like the bad guy is ever that clear-cut."

"Maybe not, but it can be." She'd never doubted North Star. The work they'd done to take down the

Sons of the Badlands hadn't always been clear-cut, but taking down a vicious, powerful group had been. And they'd done it.

Then they'd gotten involved in whatever this was. They'd stopped a weapons dealer, and now they had to stop some hit men. *Men.*

"Nate would be the other target." She frowned. Connor had said Nate had headed back home to Montana. But Holden had been dispatched to Nebraska. She might have thought that was a false alarm, or a distraction, but Shay had the whole team with Holden. He'd found something too.

"You don't think there's another hit man out there after Nate?"

"There could be. Or our guy could be offing you first, then Nate." But that didn't fully make sense. Connor hadn't been digging. Had he? "You're not lying to me? About keeping your nose clean since you've been out."

"I never saw the point. Thought it was better to move on, but…"

"But what?"

"All they'd need to know was I kept in touch. With Nate. I kept tabs. On the team. On the brass. If anyone left the military, I'd get in contact and figure out what happened just in case it matched. It never has, but I haven't fully kept my nose out of it." Connor reached out and grabbed her arm. "You've got to use that magic phone of yours and get a message to Nate."

Sabrina shook her head, then realized he wouldn't

be able to see it in the dark. "No, we have to be more careful than you've been about this."

He pulled his hand away. "Than *I've*—"

"I'm not blaming you." She cut him off quickly. "God knows I would have blown it all up, not kept my wits about me. I'm just saying, now that we know there's a real threat, we have to be more careful than a phone call. It can't be traced on my end, but I don't know about Nate's. The message we get to him has to be done as carefully and untraceably as possible."

"And if there's someone out there right now five seconds away from pulling the trigger?"

Sabrina felt a pang—fear, concern and, worst of all, some sort of empathy for Connor worried about his friend. "We have to trust Nate's abilities. Once a SEAL, always a SEAL, right? Besides, if he's been poking into this, he has to know he's in some kind of danger."

"Maybe he thinks he's been careful."

"He knows better." God, Sabrina had to hope. "Look, the one thing we know is this isn't about… speed. They've taken their time. This hit man we're after has had his ammo for days. They're setting it up so it's airtight. Luckily for you, I saved your butt by coming along when I did."

"I think an avalanche saved my butt, thanks."

She appreciated the dig. It kept them on even ground. Kept her from feeling like she needed to re-assure him. "I know it isn't easy to sit back. But we have to play this carefully. It's an operation with one goal. Keep everyone safe. Which we can't do if we panic. Here's where we rely on what we were and what we learned, and Nate's going to do the same. Nate *is* doing the same. I'm sure of it. Unless you have some reason to believe he wouldn't be?"

"No, I don't."

"Good." *Thank God.* Bad enough to have innocent blood on her hands, she'd rather not be responsible for collateral damage.

"I take it you're not still hung up on him or you'd have *some* kind of emotional response here."

The *no* was on the tip of her tongue. Even though she'd felt some guilt over the way she'd treated him, she'd accepted long ago that whatever she'd felt for Nate had been…immature. It never would have lasted even if she'd handled her injury well. But why did *Connor* need to know that? "What's it to you?"

"Nothing. Just commenting."

"Well, comment on this. I have a mission, and my personal feelings on *anything* don't matter. All that matters is we stop the hit man before he takes you or Nate out. Now, if you'll excuse me, I have a call to make."

Not that she had anywhere to go, but she walked as far away from him as she could in their little camp space, and got out her phone to call Shay.

When she got Betty, North Star's doctor, and a bunch of vague, try-again-tomorrow answers, she didn't swear or stomp or let on that she was dissatisfied.

She just went back to camp, and focused on what had to be done.

Chapter Nine

They took turns sleeping and watching out, even as the storm dumped inches of snow and icy winds on them. There was no other choice when it came to the weather, and Connor supposed there was no other choice when it came to what he now knew.

Connor figured all the revelations of the evening gave him an element of trust in Sabrina he might not have had otherwise. He knew too much. She knew too much. There was no separating now. Especially with the storm raging around them.

As for letting go of his stress and worry enough to sleep for a few hours, well, he was well versed in that. They both were well versed in that and having a few hours of rest prepared them for another long day of hiking.

They didn't talk. Not when they cleaned up the campsite or started out again. Connor quietly gave Froggy the order to track. She was trained to find bodies—live and otherwise—buried in the snow, but that didn't mean she wouldn't be able to suss out a man on a mountain when there was only the three of them.

And if the hit man *was* after him, Connor doubted he'd gone far.

So, they hiked. Through as much cover as they could find. The only difference between today and yesterday was the sky was a clear blue. The sun shone and the air was frigid since they kept climbing in elevation.

It was an absolutely breathtaking untouched world.

He wished he could enjoy it.

Instead, his mind twisted itself in circles trying to work out what he knew—or what some random hit man might *think* he knew—that could get him killed. Which led him to uncomfortable potentials Connor really didn't want to consider.

But didn't he need to? This wasn't civilian life anymore. He was being thrust back into his military one. Which meant turning off his emotions. Turning back into a soldier.

There was a time being a soldier had been natural. A time when he'd even enjoyed it. He found it no longer fit comfortably and he didn't know what to do about it except suck it up.

Which meant not being afraid of worst-case scenarios. "Nate could already be dead. And they could think he told me something."

He said it without working up to it, because he didn't know how to soften the blow of that possibility for himself. She'd been unaffected by Nate's involvement yesterday, so she either truly didn't care about her ex, or she was an excellent actress.

He didn't care either way.

But she stopped dead in her tracks as the words

seemed to sink in. "That's worst-case scenario," she said carefully. Like she was weighing every word before she said it.

"Yeah, it is. But it makes more sense to me than anything." Connor shut off the part of himself that wanted to pre-grieve. No use before he knew anything. "Why come after me first?"

"Because you're the easier target? As a warning? Especially if you don't actually know anything. You don't know how deep Nate is into this."

"It'd help if we did. If we got in contact with him."

She was walking again, trudging through the snow with that overly heavy pack. But they were past the casual bickering and sniping they'd started off with. This was serious now.

"I'm working on it," Sabrina said. She didn't sound so much defensive as…irritated.

"You need to work faster."

"Look, if he's already dead, too late. If he's not, we have to be careful we don't lead the hit man to him. Are you sure they'd be able to find him?"

"They found me."

"You work in the public, Connor. I bet your pretty face is splashed all over your SAR group's website. What does Nate do?"

Connor hesitated to answer, because it was irritating she had a point. "He's at a ranch in his hometown," he grumbled.

"A ranch? I mean obviously I knew Nate before you, but back in the day his plans were definitely not go home to the family ranch in nowhere Montana."

"It's not his family's. It's…a ranch for injured military guys. A rehab type facility."

"Oh, so you're telling me he's *surrounded* by other military guys and you're all alone? Gee, I wonder which one I'd off first."

"Because you can predict how a hit man, potentially working for the US military to off its former soldiers, would think, act and plan?"

"First, it's not the military. Not saying the guys involved might not be *in* the military, but there's no way the brass sent a hit man after you when you don't even know anything. Unless they themselves were involved in something shady."

"You so sure about that?"

"Based on what I know? Yeah. I am. Just like I know my next suggestion is going to sound crazy, but I think we should—"

But her words were cut off by a sharp, decisive bark from Froggy. Connor grabbed Sabrina's shoulder and pushed her down into a crouch. They both had their guns ready, eyes scanning the blinding white around them.

"I don't see anything."

"She might just smell a track, a campsite or something like that. But we'll want to proceed with caution."

Sabrina sent Froggy a sidelong glance. "You don't want to send her forward first."

"Worried about my dog, Sabrina?"

She scowled. "Just saying. If she can give you some idea of direction, I'll go first. Maybe I can pick up some tracks."

"Just a big old softie, aren't you?"

"Trying to protect your dog here. You really want to make fun of me over it?"

"Kind of." And only because the fact she'd care about Froggy's well-being made him feel a little too soft toward this woman currently upending his life.

Or saving it.

Yeah, he wasn't going to think like that. He crouched next to Froggy, stroked her head, and murmured a few commands to her. The dog sniffed the ground, began to catch a scent. Connor held her back. "This way."

Sabrina went ahead, searching the ground with an interminable attention to every detail. He'd never seen her so careful or still. Each move was measured. Controlled. All that energy usually pumping off of her contained.

It was fascinating. Way too appealing. Especially when despite the layers and packs, it was no challenge to imagine the lithe, athletic body beneath.

"Kind of a dead end here. But look." She pointed ahead of them a few yards. There was a small cave mouth at the base of two boulders.

"That'd be a good place to camp. Especially last night."

"It'd also be a good place to hide right now," Sabrina replied. "You got a light handy?"

Connor nodded and pulled the flashlight from its loop on his backpack. She held out a hand for it, but he ignored her and turned the light on himself, inching toward the cave mouth. He stayed on one side of the opening, and Sabrina stayed on the other, weapon at the ready.

She kept Froggy behind her, and again Connor had to pretend that sort of thing didn't matter to him. He crouched, inched into the cave as soundlessly as possible.

The air was colder in here, but there was no wind, so it was definitely protected. Damp, but if you had the right gear that'd be okay. His light swept carefully over the dark space.

"Clear," Connor said. The opening was small enough he didn't see anywhere someone could hide. And the remains of a campfire were in the middle, long since put out. Connor crouched next to it as Sabrina and Froggy entered the cave too.

He touched the fire remnants. "Cold."

"Must have been up earlier than us."

"It's cold enough in here it wouldn't take long to cool the embers off. Or he could have had a fire last night and not this morning. A lot of options." Connor sat back on his haunches and considered. He didn't really know where to go from here. They could keep following the guy, but it seemed like they'd continue to be just out of reach.

Until the hit man decided to make the hit, he supposed. "What was your crazy plan?"

"I'm not sure he knows that the people he shot at are me and you. Me, maybe. You? Why would he?"

"He knew I wanted to rescue him."

"Sure, but would he assume you'd keep searching

for him? When it was obvious he'd run away on his own two feet?"

"Then where's he going? Higher and higher. That's not the way to me."

"No, it's not. Not to you *here*." Sabrina agreed. Too easily. "But wouldn't this, in a roundabout way, lead back to your cabin?"

Connor tried not to jerk at how right on she was. Because if he thought about the mountain terrain, the direction they were going, the easy thing would have been to get to his cabin the way they'd *left* his cabin. But going this way would also lead to the same general area, but with a lot of tree cover.

"So, what are you suggesting we do?" Connor asked, still staring at the blackened remains of a fire.

"Stop chasing him higher. Stop exhausting ourselves. I say we go back to your cabin and wait for him to come for us."

"Stop chasing. Wait for him to come for us."

"Yes, those are the words I just said." The way Connor repeated them, like they were so foreign he didn't even know what they meant, almost made her laugh.

"You're the one who—"

"The original plan was to follow him, stop him, yeah. Then I figured out *you* were the target. Things have changed. What do we get out of chasing him?"

"Knowing where he is."

"We know he's after you. Isn't that enough? We go back to your cabin. Hunker down for the duration. Set up some traps of our own. Maybe even convince him we *don't* know he's after you. That you were never out here chasing him." She'd have a chance to get a real hold of Shay or *someone* at North Star who could send her some backup.

"He saw us. He has to know—"

"At best, he saw two figures. If he'd had any kind of scope or binoculars, one of us would be dead."

Connor shook his head. "You know that isn't true. *You* knew something was about to happen. That's why I'm not dead. You knew something was wrong and pushed me down."

An odd satisfaction swept over her. She didn't need external praise. Didn't need anyone else to see she'd done her job and tell her, but it was weirdly…nice that he understood she had been the one to save his life. "Maybe."

"Maybe," he snorted irritably. "Yes, that is what happened." He stood up from the crouch, though he had to tilt his head to one side not to hit it on the cave ceiling.

"Okay, that's what happened. Still, that doesn't mean he knows that you were his original target. If he knows who I am, he might have thought you were someone working with me. There's a lot of what-ifs. But if he is after *you*, and I don't think that's one of our ifs, following him doesn't do much for us. He'll always have higher ground, a head start, and the upper hand. Why not make him come to us?"

"So, you want to go back to my cabin and hide?"

"I want to go back to your cabin and lay a trap, Connor. It's tactical. I wouldn't mind being tactical *and* warm, would you?" She looked at the dog. She could probably handle it, what with the fur and training and all, but Sabrina couldn't help but feel sorry for the animal. "I think Froggy and I are in the same boat."

He huffed out a breath. "And what if we go back to my cabin. Fortify, lay a trap, whatever. What prevents him from going off to take out Nate?"

"Time? Distance? At some point, he's going to figure out we've figured him out, which means he'll realize he's got to get rid of us before we can tell Nate he's a target too."

"Which you refuse to do."

"I don't refuse to do it. I just know we have to do it carefully, and you know, I can be a lot more careful getting messages if I'm in a house with electricity."

"That's *if* all our guessing is right."

She wanted to pummel him, but she took a deep breath and slowly let it out. She'd keep her calm. She had to. "Yeah. Sometimes you've got to take decisive action on what information you've got. Maybe it's wrong. But what's the other option?"

He was quiet for a long while, his gaze on the dog standing between them. Sabrina didn't know if he was thinking about her, or just thinking in general, but she waited. Pestering him into agreeing with her wasn't going to work. So, she bit her tongue and waited.

She really tried to wait.

"Look. If we go back to your cabin, I can probably get some backup. Not right away or anything, but maybe a team. We could surround the place, and—"

"A *team*?"

Sabrina tried not to wince. "Yeah, a team."

"Why don't you have a team right now?" he demanded angrily. Though it was undercut by the way he had to keep his head to the side to stand in this cave.

Sabrina thought about Holden. She didn't know anything about the lead he'd found. She'd think it had something to do with Nate, but why Nebraska? "Was there anyone else in on this thing with you and Nate? Anyone else who would be a target?"

"Yeah, change the subject," he muttered irritably, but he eventually answered her question. "We had a team of sixteen, but we worked in partners. Nate was mine. No one else was discharged when we were. It seems unlikely they've got a hit man out there trying to take out an entire navy SEAL team. Especially when a good half of us are still SEALs."

"And you know that because…?"

"Because I keep track."

"Uh-huh."

"It's not the same as digging into what happened."

"Isn't it?"

"What about this *team*, Sabrina?"

"They're currently occupied. But by the time we get back to your cabin, who knows?"

"Who knows. Shouldn't you know?"

"Look, I'm not going to stand here watching you get a crick in your neck while we argue about this. My plan is to go back to your cabin and make our guy come to us. You got a better one?"

He stood there glowering, there was no other word for it, and even with his head cocked at an awkward angle that glower had some *effect*. Too bad it was all south of the border effects.

"Come on, Connor. Let's go set a trap."

Chapter Ten

Connor hated feeling out of his element. Like he was walking through some maze he didn't know all the parts to. But Sabrina had a point with one thing—he didn't have a better plan.

Besides, if they got back to his cabin, *he* could get his own message to Nate. Regardless of all her concern. Back home, he'd have access to communications and making some of his own decisions, with or without Sabrina's agreement.

So, it made sense to leave the cave and hike back to his cabin. Or if not *sense*, it was the only option. They could keep hiking after the hit man, but to what end? A standoff they couldn't control? A trap of the hit man's own?

"He won't expect this, you know," Sabrina pointed out as they hiked through the quietly sunny day. The wind was still bitterly cold, but only blew occasionally. It might have been an enjoyable walk.

If not for all the impending death hanging around them.

But she was right. This was not the expected response. The guy had to know he was being tracked. A sudden about-face would leave him confused.

But Connor wasn't fully convinced that would work in their favor even as he led Sabrina back to his cabin. "Won't he know we're trying to trap *him*?"

"Maybe." Sabrina shrugged next to him as if she didn't have a care in the world. "But as long as he's here, playing our game, that means he's nowhere near Nate. Doesn't it?"

"There could be two."

"There could be." Sabrina took a deep breath, squinted at the world around him. "Look. I work for this private group, right? I was sent here looking for this hit man. It's a long, complicated story, but basically I was tracking the ammo for this gun, and very little information from another group. But it wasn't just me or this guy. Another one of my teammates was sent to Nebraska to track another shipment of ammo. Another hit man."

"Nebraska? But—"

"There *are* two hit men. The other one is in Nebraska. So, he's either after someone else, or Nate isn't in danger yet."

"That doesn't make sense. Nate wouldn't be hard to track." He'd gone to his hometown. Surely that would make him even easier pickings than Connor himself. "Maybe there's a third."

"Maybe there is, but he'd be using different ammo and a different MO? Doesn't add up. Maybe this doesn't all make sense big picture, but small picture? That's what we've got to work with."

She spoke and moved with a confidence Connor couldn't find within himself. Had he gone soft? Was that the price of civilian life?

"How'd you get involved in this group?" Maybe if he understood her, her group, this whole *operation*, he might find that confidence again. That sure footing. Because it wasn't about trust. He had to search and rescue with people he didn't necessarily *trust*, but he understood what both parties were after. He knew all about their training.

Sabrina was a big question mark. And she'd probably stay that way.

"You don't have to worry about my group. We're on the up-and-up. I promise you that."

"My life and my friend's life are on the line here. Why should I just trust some stranger's promise? Would you?"

She seemed to ponder that. "No, I wouldn't. It'd take a lot for me to trust anything. I get it. And this goes better if we trust each other." She blew out a breath. "Getting involved with my group goes back to when I got hurt. The recovery would take too long to keep my place in my SEAL class. I could have stuck it out, worked hard and maybe stayed in the navy, but…I'd wanted to be a SEAL. There was no runner-up that would have satisfied me at the time. I was young. I was angry. And I'd lost the one goal I'd ever set myself, aside from get the hell off my dad's farm."

He listened, tucking away the details he didn't know if she was purposefully giving him to build that layer of trust, or if she was just letting things slip. But she wasn't the kind of person who let things slip, so he had to believe the first.

She mentioned her father's farm, she mentioned how much the SEALs meant, because she was allowing him to understand this enough to believe her. To trust her.

Sneaky, because if they really trusted each other, going their own way without the other knowing about it would come with guilt.

"Your dad's farm. Not your family farm?"

She laughed. Bitterly. "It was never mine. Some people have families, I suppose. The real kind. Some people are just separate entities sharing the same space until one can escape."

Connor couldn't say he knew what that was like, so he kept his mouth shut.

"My crappy childhood isn't the point. Except that it's why the SEALs was so important to me. I didn't just want to escape and the military was there. I wanted to do something big. I wanted to be *elite*. A middle finger to the old man. So, losing that, it was a failure on a lot of levels, and this may come as a surprise to you as I'm such a retiring, rule-following paragon of womanhood now."

Connor snorted.

"But I blew up my entire life. Top to bottom. Nate tried to be sweet about it. Which was the worst thing to do, for me, in that situation. So, I kicked him to the curb, and I just…took off. Didn't realize I was headed back to that godforsaken farm until I was crossing the Kansas border. Since I wasn't that much of a masoch- ist, I took a sharp left north instead and ended up in

South Dakota. Got a job at a gas station. Got in fights at bars at night to work out all that anger. Picked a fight with the wrong guy."

"Surprised to hear you admit you could come up against the wrong guy."

"Oh, I kicked his butt, more or less, don't get me wrong. Just turned out this guy, who I'd just sliced with a broken bottle, had sort of been there done that in terms of being the young moron on the wrong path. He offered me a job."

She laughed, and it wasn't bitter. It was like she was recounting a fond memory. Of slicing a man with a broken bottle. Yeah, that seemed about right with this woman.

"Didn't believe him at first. Obviously. But he kept pestering me, got his boss to come meet me." She adjusted her pack a little as they walked. "He was… Older. Not old enough to be my dad, but had that… vibe, you know? Like when you have a horrible dad, you always have a vision of what a good one looks like, and he just…fit. Not paternal. He was straightforward and gruff, but said he'd done his research and thought I'd be a good fit. Believed in my skills. They both did. They had all this faith in what I could give to their group."

Connor could tell, even as she hurried to keep talking, that had been one of the most meaningful parts of her life. Not anything warm or fuzzy, but someone believing in her skills.

"Still didn't believe them, but I figured I could give it a shot and keep one foot out the door. Maybe even fight some people without getting myself thrown in jail. So, I did the first mission, then the second. Eventually, we did some real good in the world and I realized I believed them. And I belonged. And I knew, fully down-in-the-gut knew we were doing the right thing. And helping people."

She cleared her throat, sliding him a look. It wasn't calculating or anything. It was almost...embarrassed. It was that more than anything that made him believe she was giving him the full, unvarnished truth.

"There. Now you have my story. Sabrina Killian in a nutshell. Your turn."

He didn't have to tell her. That much Connor knew. And if he kept himself somewhat separate, or if he even made some stuff up to lie to her with, he'd have an easier time doing what he wanted to do.

But it felt wrong.

CONNOR DIDN'T DO a good job of hiding his thoughts. It was all over his face. She could practically *hear* him thinking, wondering if he should lie to her.

He could. Sabrina had faith that she'd know if he did. She also had a pretty good dose of faith that he'd tell her the truth. Guy was that true-blue Captain America type.

"My parents are pretty decent. Had too many kids for what they could afford, but they loved us. I didn't leave to escape, but I did leave to make something of myself. I get that. I wanted to make them proud."

It gave her a pang. Something like longing. Silly, to still wish she'd had what she never would.

"And you did," she supplied for him.

"I did. In fairness, I could have done just about anything and made them proud. Still, being something they could brag about felt good. And I got to be away from that crowded house, send some money home and see the world. Navy life and then SEAL life wasn't a joy or a picnic, but I felt like I was doing something... good. At first."

The *at first* surprised her when she didn't think he would. When she thought she had him pegged. "You're not saying you got disillusioned?"

"The missions I went on didn't leave room for much else. It's not like what you said about your...group. I didn't know I was fighting for the right side. It's too muddied. Too complicated. So, yeah, I was feeling a little disillusioned there. But I had a mission, and I was going to complete it. Do my time. Do the right thing."

Yeah, he was a man who would—always—do the right thing. She was a little surprised he'd been good friends with Nate. Nate was a good guy and all, but he'd had an edge to him. Like her, he'd had some...willingness to bend the rules. To follow their own drummer beats.

"I've told you the story. Nate finds this civilian he thinks is going to help, but instead the guy takes everything Nate tells him and gives it to his insurgent group." Connor's eyebrows drew together, even as he kept marching along. "It wouldn't have been enough for a serious intel breach. It just...wouldn't have. I was there. I would know."

Sabrina thought about it, like she'd been turning it

over in her mind all night. "I have a theory. And that supports it. Maybe there was nothing you and Nate did wrong. Maybe someone else, higher up, was doing something wrong. And they framed you two."

"To what end?"

"To make it look like they'd found the bad guy. To get you out of the way. So, they could keep doing the bad thing. Your discharges didn't make sense. Nate's not the kind of guy who just accepts that—especially since he was the one trusting this civilian, and you got caught up in it. Nate's warped sense of responsibility wouldn't let that rest."

"Warped?"

She shook her head. She wouldn't argue semantics when her theory made *sense*. "Nate gets close to the truth, and he has to be taken out. Or threatened, depending on who the bad guy is and what they want. Silence. Cooperation."

"I don't know why they'd go after me first."

"No, I don't either."

"We have to get in touch with Nate. We *have* to."

"I agree." She still wanted to do it carefully, but the truth she believed at this point was that Connor was some kind of target because of Nate. Which meant getting an understanding of what Nate knew. What he'd done.

"You agree? No buts?"

"I still want to work out the best way to do it. The most careful way. If I'm right, Connor, Nate knows. He knows exactly the kind of danger he's in. What he might not know is that you're in danger too."

Connor glanced at her, a considering and not completely kind perusal. "You don't want to split his focus," he said flatly.

She didn't understand the tone of voice. Or the way her chest pinched. "It's not that simple."

"None of this is simple," Connor muttered.

"Exactly." She blew out a breath. "We have to—"

But Connor's arm shot out, stopping her progress. He lifted his nose to the air, sniffed. Sabrina watched him in confusion, but took a deep sniff of mountain air too…except it wasn't just the smell of snow and pine needles.

"Smoke," Sabrina said, a shiver of fear working its way through her. "He's close?"

"That isn't campfire smoke." Connor jogged forward and climbed up onto a large boulder. She tried to follow, but she didn't have the same kind of climbing skill, and he'd left Froggy down here with her.

"What is it?" she demanded, rather than try to scramble up after him and leave the dog on her own.

He didn't answer her right away. He climbed down from the rock first. When he stood face-to-face with her, she saw a bleakness and a fury that had that shiver of fear working through her again.

"It's my cabin," he said, his voice gruff.

"What?"

"I can't see it from here, but I can see where the smoke is coming from. I'm willing to bet it's my damn cabin that's on fire." He started marching forward, long strides she had to scurry to keep up with.

"Connor."

"He set fire to my damn cabin," Connor said, shaking off her hand when she tried to grab him and stop his quickening pace.

"Connor, we can't go there."

He whirled on her. But all that fury and rage on his face disappeared after a few seconds. Like he'd carefully locked it all away. When he spoke, it was with a carefulness that made her...cold. "All my stuff. Froggy's food. I need—"

"We can't go back," Sabrina said, not sure why her voice was so *gentle*. "It's either a trap or a warning. Either way... Our hit man didn't get back to your cabin *that* fast. Did he?"

Connor seemed to consider. "We're still miles off. He'd had to have... No, he couldn't have gotten there *and* set a fire." He closed his eyes as if that could block out the bad news.

"There's more than one," Sabrina said out loud, even though she knew he'd figured it out himself. "Our hit man has backup. We can't go back. We have to..."

"Run away? Hide?" Connor demanded angrily.

She felt for him, she really did. Which wasn't comfortable...all this *empathy*. "We have to be smart. We have to be careful. For ourselves. For Nate." And she had to get rid of all these soft feelings careening around in her chest. "There's got to be somewhere we can go and...recalculate."

But he wasn't listening. She could tell he was somewhere else. Somewhere she understood. An impotent rage at things that were already done. He stood there, looking like fury personified, and her heart softened.

Very much against her will.

Chapter Eleven

Connor couldn't remember the last time he'd had to fight so hard against the rising tide of fury. Some nameless, faceless nobodies had set fire to his cabin. Though he couldn't actually see his cabin due to the rises and falls of the earth and how far away they were, he knew that rising smoke could only be that one thing.

He knew.

There was nothing else to set fire to around there, and setting a fire in the snow-covered woods would require so much work it wouldn't be worth it. But a house fire could be set from the inside out.

It was as senseless and frustrating as his sudden and confusing discharge had been, but not having to serve his final enlistment year had been something of a relief too. He'd been done with the SEALs, with the military, but was going to gut it out. Do his duty. Because it was the right thing to do. Nevertheless, there'd been no grief at it being ended early. Only confusion.

He wasn't done with his cabin. With his things. This was personal, beyond any of the offensive things that had happened to him in his discharge from the navy. This was personal, and there would be grief.

Sabrina touched his arm. Gently. Her expression was…sympathetic. It was the antithesis of everything she'd been up to this point and that… It wasn't good. It loosened things in his chest he couldn't afford to loosen.

"I'm sorry," she said, and her voice sounded like it belonged to someone else. Someone soft and kind. "Losing your cabin is…"

He stepped away from her hand. He looked down at Froggy to keep his focus where it needed to be. "My cabin isn't accessible by car or truck," he said, ignoring Sabrina's apologies. "They would have had to have something all-terrain. And since they're at my cabin, they've likely either destroyed my ATV or used it for themselves. I keep a Jeep at SAR headquarters in Wilson. Hiking there would take…days. At best."

She nodded, as if she understood both what he was saying, and what he was doing by putting some distance between them. "I'd say we could radio your SAR buddies, but—"

"No, they stay away. No one's getting shot at over me." Though he had some concerns that if news of his cabin burning down got out, they'd start looking for him. Iona definitely would. He needed to get a message to her to hold her off, but first they needed a plan.

"Any other cabins around here?" Sabrina asked.

"Here and there, but they've got people. They're too far and… Wait." Connor cut himself off as he remembered one place that might work. "There's a ranger cabin. Not close, but walkable." He eyed the sky, the area they were in. "We can probably get there before afternoon. The park rangers use it for summer interns so it should still be empty for a few more weeks. Not sure what kind of provisions it'll have, but we can set up there and figure things out."

"Lead the way."

He did. At a pace just shy of reckless. But the sooner they got there, the sooner they could really sort this mess out. Contact Nate. Tell Iona to stay the hell away.

Would she? Connor had his doubts. So, he had to find a way to convince her he didn't need her help.

"What about the fire?" Sabrina asked while they hiked. When they were higher up, the smoke was visible, even though they were going in the opposite direction now. "Do you think emergency services will be called? Or that your friends might come looking for you?"

"News of the fire should take some time to spread. I'm pretty isolated. So, unless these guys set the fire and called the fire department, it's likely going to go out on its own before anyone notices. Especially with all this new snow and the avalanche. Hikers won't be out to see and call."

"You're *that* isolated?"

"Yeah."

"Interesting choice for a guy who says he's got a nice family."

It was none of her business, but it seemed they'd reached this place where they weren't strangers anymore. They knew each other's backgrounds. Motivations, to an extent. Hopefully it would help them work together, trust each other, because this was getting messier and more complicated by the minute.

"I didn't want to lie when I got home. Not to anyone's face. I'm not that great at it when it comes to people I care about. So, I found this place. I found SAR training. By the time my fake injuries would have healed, and I could have gone home without too many lies, I found I liked my solitude. I loved what I was doing. I visit my family when I want. They come to Jackson Hole in the summer. It works." It did, and because it did, a heavy weight of worry settled itself on his chest. Connor sucked in a breath, tried to think rationally. "You don't think they'd get roped into this, do you?"

"Obviously I can't promise you that, but if you've kept your distance? I don't see any reason to kill a bunch of innocent civilians. They wanted to scare you, they'd have done it already. You're a target, the kind they want to kill, not scare, because they must think you know something. They have to think you know something."

"We have to get in touch with Nate," Connor muttered. Knowing what she would say. "We have to know what he has. What he knows. What these people might think *I* know. Because if he doesn't know anything…"

"I think I've got an idea on that score. But I need to use my computer. How long do you think it'll take us to get to this cabin?"

"Good Lord, you're carrying a computer in there?"

"Small one. For emergencies. This counts."

He was going to question her about wifi, then thought better of it. If she got cell service out here, chances were her group had some sort of futuristic way to connect to the internet. "A good three hours. But even if we slow down, not more than four."

"Okay. And you really don't think anyone's going to know about the fire for that long?"

"It's unlikely. Highly unlikely."

Sabrina nodded. "Then let's book it."

Connor agreed, but that didn't mean he was going to wait for the cabin to hear how a computer was going to put them in touch with Nate any more untraceably than a phone call.

"So, what's the idea?"

"I've got a program on my computer that can send untraceable emails. If I can figure out a way to get Nate's email address, one he'll actually check, and use some kind of coded language to let him know what's going on, it's possible we can get a message to him— even one that's intercepted—that no one will think twice about. Something like that. But I've got to fiddle with my program."

"Nate's not big on email."

"Yeah, that's part of the problem. But maybe… someone he's living with is? I just need to sit down and do like thirty minutes of research and maybe we can get a lead on how to tug that line without putting him in danger's way. Or you."

"I'm already in danger's way apparently. You aren't worried about you? Or your group?"

"I'm a ghost, Con. Even if they find my name, they

won't know who I work for or where I came from. But like you said, you have family. You have connections. So, we don't want them looking any harder at you than a double tap, you're dead."

He laughed. Couldn't help it. All the sympathy and kindness was gone and *thank God*. Her irreverence made him feel far more sturdy than her *emotion*. "You're a constant comfort, Sabrina."

She sent him that quicksilver grin. "I try."

SABRINA DIDN'T BOTHER wishing her pack was twenty pounds lighter. She didn't curse at the ache in her back. She didn't even grumble at Connor for this never-ending hike to some *supposedly* abandoned cabin.

It damn well better be after all this.

But she swallowed it all down, kept her complaints to herself, because she'd made her heavy pack bed, and now it was time to lie in it.

"Let's trade packs for an hour," Connor said. Casually. Deceptively casual.

"Not on your life," she returned, focusing on her breathing so it didn't sound all huffy and puffy like it actually was.

"You're slowing down," he said, and this time his voice was not casual. It was pointed.

And right on target, which stung her pride. She'd once carried heavier rucksacks across much more difficult terrain, but it wasn't something she had to do often with North Star. "I carry my weight."

"Stubbornly. With no regard as to if it's the smart thing to do."

"Pretty much."

He grumbled something under his breath, but he let it go. Sabrina wasn't letting herself check the time. It would just depress her how few hours they'd been at it, but she followed the path of the sun in the sky. It was past noon. They had to be getting close.

She still hadn't heard from anyone at North Star, and that made her edgier than she'd like. What she really wanted to do was get in contact with Elsie and get her advice on how to email safely, or even have Elsie do it. But if she was working on Holden's side of things, Sabrina was just going to have to trust her own instincts there.

Which made her nervous. Which made her irritable. She wanted to snap at Connor, but he looked a bit like he was about to snap himself. Too many unanswered questions.

They needed to talk to Nate. She should be thinking about that and only that. Though, she had to admit, watching Connor's butt was a nice distraction from the way her pack dug into her shoulders.

"There," Connor said, looking like some sort of god standing on a rock, pointing off into the distance. "See it?"

She climbed up on top of the rock with him and Froggy. She could make out a small, brown structure if she squinted. "How far you think that is?"

He eyed her. "Far enough."

Sabrina huffed out an irritated breath. "*Fine*. You win." She unsnapped her pack, shrugged it off and handed it to him. He handed her his, and they worked to adjust the straps on both their new packs.

Once it was on her back she scowled. "This isn't that much lighter."

"But lighter," he said. "Come on now, let's make good progress this last mile."

"*Mile.*" Sabrina allowed herself one childish moan, but kept up with him and the dog as they hiked the remaining distance. The building they reached was small and clearly old. The yard around it was overgrown with grasses and summer wildflowers. There was a towering pine tree to the side that gave off considerable shade.

The porch creaked precariously as Connor walked up the stairs. He opened the storm door, then looked back at her. "I could break it down, but I'm going to go out on a limb and guess you probably know how to pick a lock."

She smiled at him and batted her eyelashes. "Your faith in me is *so* sweet." She dug the Swiss Army knife out of her pocket and then crouched next to the door and got to work.

When she swung the door open without any damage to the knob, she gestured Connor inside dramatically. "*Entre.*"

"My hero," he said, deadpan. Which made her laugh. He stepped inside first, and she followed, eagerly dropping the pack off of her sore shoulders.

Connor did the same, then bent down to unclip Froggy's leash. Inside the house was dark, and a flip of the light switch did not do anything to alleviate dark or cold.

"Electricity must be shut off," Connor said. "I'll see if I can do anything about that, but for now figure out your computer stuff. I'm going to water and feed Froggy, then put together something for us to eat."

"Back to giving orders?" she asked, but it was a good-natured dig, because she was already pulling her computer out of her pack. Finding a way to carefully contact Nate was now her number one goal. "You said he's at a ranch? Or a rehab facility or something."

"Yeah. Both. In Blue Valley, Montana."

"I'll see what I can do." She tuned everything else out. Connor talking to Froggy. The lights suddenly coming on. She focused only on finding this rehab center—easy enough—and then a way to get a message that would be delivered to a man at such a place.

Once she thought she had a reasonable target to get a message to Nate, she opened the program Elsie had installed onto her computer a while ago. Sabrina hadn't fully listened to what the program did, but she knew whatever email she sent—usually to North Star staff—couldn't be hacked or traced.

Now, when she sent something to North Star, she knew it was going to a similarly safe program. Sending this email to Revival Ranch's contact email meant that someone could and would read it. But as long as they didn't track it back to North Star, or Sabrina's current location, it should be fine.

So, why did she feel so nervous?

Big stakes. Nerves were par for the course.

Before she figured out how to code a message to Nate, she wrote an email to Elsie about what she was doing with the hopes Elsie would be able to hack in and fix any mistakes Sabrina might make.

She thought about emailing Shay, or sending her yet another text, but she mentally talked herself out of it. She'd called. She'd left messages. Betty knew she was trying to get in contact with everyone. If no one had gotten back to her, they were busy.

She refused to think about that meaning Holden was in significant trouble.

She leaned back and rolled her shoulders. A bowl appeared next to her, steaming and full of a hearty-looking stew.

Sabrina glanced up at Connor. "Got a beer to go with it, sweetie?"

"Cute," he said, rolling his eyes. He went back to the kitchenette and brought another bowl of stew to the table. He sat next to her and gestured at the computer. "So, what have you come up with?"

"We're going to have it be from me." She took a spoonful of stew. Clearly some canned concoction, but good enough. "That way he might be curious to read it. And it makes sure nothing connects to you that someone might trace."

"Okay. So start off with something super personal. Any cute nicknames from your relationship?"

Sabrina pulled a face. "Don't be a weirdo."

"Apparently your pet name for me is sweetie. Surely you had one for Nate."

She laughed, and knew that's what he'd wanted. To

loosen her up some. She appreciated it, not that she'd tell him that. "No nicknames. I used to call him Nathan to tick him off."

"There you go. Be yourself and start with that."

"I don't *always* try to tick people off."

"Don't you?"

She looked over at him and couldn't stop herself from grinning. "Only the special ones."

He shook his head, but his mouth curved. She could tell he was trying to fight the grin, the amusement, but it didn't work. He took a bite of stew, and she was still staring for some unknown reason. Maybe it was because his eyes had a measure of warmth in them, and that was a first. One that had things fluttering around in her chest and pulsing dangerously lower.

She looked back down at the email, focus shattered. But she started typing, anything that came into her head. *Press on*, she told herself.

Definitely don't dwell on any heart racing or *sudden shivers*.

ing, but she took it anyway, fighting with everything she was to keep the tremor out of her hands.

God, what had that *been*? No one had ever kissed her with all that… What? She didn't even have a word for it.

Her phone began ringing again. She cleared her throat. "Killian," she answered, irritated her voice was still rough.

"Sabrina. Thank God."

"Shay?" Relief would have flooded her, but her boss's voice didn't sound all that steady.

"Listen. I don't know what you've found, but Holden's mission led him to one of the names of the hit man's target. Unfortunately, we know there's another hit man and another name out there. We only got intermediaries. I don't know when we'll get the second name, but your assignment is the first one. Listen carefully, the first target's name is Connor Lindstrom. I haven't had time to—"

"Shay."

"Sabrina. Don't interrupt. Time—"

"Shay. I'm *with* Connor Lindstrom. He's the SAR guy. The one I told you about."

"Oh. Oh… I… Well."

Sabrina wished she could be amused she'd surprised Shay of all people, but there were too many things jangling around inside of her to find any humor. "We figured out he was the target just last night, and we're pretty sure we know the second target. His name's Nathan Averly. He's in Blue Valley, Montana. I need Elsie to—"

"Els was hurt, Sabrina."

"Elsie?" Sabrina's heart clutched painfully at how grave Shay sounded. "Hurt? But how? Why?"

"We had her doing some computer work on-site. Unfortunately she got caught in the middle a little bit. She's going to be fine, but for right now she's in the hospital."

Sabrina closed her eyes. It was both relief and pain. Elsie would be fine. That was great. But she was no agent. She was IT. She should be safe, not in the hospital. "Did anyone else get hurt?"

"We're all okay, more or less. We'll give you more details soon, but there are more strings to tie up here. I needed to get you that name. And you're... You're with him. Geez. That's a stroke of luck."

Sabrina wished she felt lucky. "His cabin got burned down. We're laying low. I've made careful contact with the second target. We need more information from him to understand who's after them."

"We'll get you more information on that angle as soon as we can. Are you safe? Can you sit tight for a few?"

"We're good for tonight. But I need someone to dig on Nate without anyone knowing they're digging. I need..." She needed Elsie, damn it. "I don't want us digging to come back on anybody. Or let them know we're after them and have whoever is doing this escalate. I might have names, but I don't feel close to figuring this out. Do you know where the second hit man is?"

"No. We know there was an ammo tradeoff a day ago. So the person who picked it up here in Nebraska isn't the shooter. But that does mean they've had a day to get to this Blue Valley, Montana."

Sabrina wouldn't allow herself to panic. It was better than a hit man already being there, but not by much. "Someone could have gotten to Montana by now."

"Yes. You've warned the second target?"

"I've sent a message. I don't know that he's gotten it." Maybe she shouldn't have been so careful. Maybe warning Nate ASAP would have been the better course of action.

"We'll clean things up here. I'll get a team to Blue Valley. You focus on the hit man after Connor Lindstrom."

"We need to know why, Shay. We need to figure this out. It's got something to do with their time together in the navy SEALs. The way they were discharged wasn't on the up-and-up."

"Got it. Look, I know Elsie's the best, but one of her IT team can handle this. I'm sure they can. So, we'll get one of them on it. We'll get a team to Montana ASAP, and I'll get you some backup."

Sabrina eyed Connor. He hadn't moved. Perhaps not a muscle. He stood there like some mountain of immovable stone. "I'm not saying no to backup, but we're good here. So, we're the last priority. As long as we're here, and they're burning down his cabin, they're going to stay put and look for us." Whoever *they* were. How many and what skills and weapons was a mystery, but Sabrina had to believe she and Connor could handle it. For now.

"All right. I've got to take care of things here. I'll be in touch. Stay safe."

"You too." The line went dead. Sabrina found herself delaying pulling the phone away from her ear. Found herself...not quite ready to face Connor and what had transpired before that phone call.

But she was not a coward. She wasn't going to be nervous over a kiss that hadn't gone the way she'd planned. "Don't know how much you heard, but we got some information. Mostly intermediary stuff or confirming what we already know. I think the best course of action is to sit tight here tonight and then hope we've got some more to go on in the morning. My group will be sending a team to Nate, so we don't have to worry too much about him. A warning and backup. It's the best we can do."

He didn't say anything to that, and she found no matter how she told herself not to be a coward, she couldn't quite force herself to look at him. "So, we've eaten. Now we should rest." She started walking past him to find if there was a bedroom or, please God, two separate rooms to sleep in.

But as she tried to brush past him, his hand shot out and grabbed her arm. Hard.

"What was it you said to me? Don't disappoint me by playing coy?"

Both his grasp and words irritated her enough to snap her gaze to meet his. She had a million brilliant, cutting rejoinders on the tip of her tongue. She did, she *really* did.

But he used all that strength to jerk her against him, haul her up and crush his mouth to hers, and the words just melted away.

Everything did.

Chapter Thirteen

Connor hadn't meant to find himself back here. He'd meant to prove something. That he could be as aggressive and flippant as she. That he wasn't a coward who was just going to pretend the first kiss hadn't happened. No, things weren't going to go down that way.

But he hadn't meant to kiss her again. It was too dangerous. Just a little touch, and a verbal jab that would leave her off kilter. That had been the plan. He'd been certain it would work.

But she'd looked at him with all that fire, and she hadn't fought him off like he knew she could have. And he just...

Went with it.

Whatever she'd been thinking when she'd originally kissed him, he didn't know, but it had unlocked something inside of him. Because here, with her mouth meeting his kiss for kiss, nip for nip, he didn't think. *Couldn't* think.

It was just her and lust and greed and absolutely no thought to anything beyond having his hands on her. His mouth on her. *Having* her.

"I want you," he found himself saying against her mouth, hands tangled in her hair as she wound herself around him—arms banded around his neck, legs vised around his waist.

"So have me."

She was wrapped around him so he only had to shift his grip on her to lift her up, walk her deeper into the cabin.

"Bedroom somewhere," he muttered, his brain feeling a bit like it had been fried. He was okay with that as long as her body kept pressed against him, all that heat, all that strength.

He stumbled into a dark room, and only bothered to find a light switch because if he was going to be this stupid, he was damn well going to enjoy it. He flipped the switch and headed straight for the bed, never quite taking his mouth from hers.

How could he? Here was power and he wanted all he could drink of it. He dropped her to the bed, and before he could follow her hands were busy pulling his shirt over his head. He accommodated her, then pulled her shirt off. They stripped each other, touching every inch of skin exposed like two people lost in the desert finding water after days.

She was perfect. Lean and toned. Soft, with all that hair. He couldn't keep his hands out of it. Couldn't seem to take his mouth off her. Dimly he was aware this was a *terrible* idea, and they had far more important things to busy themselves with.

But her hands closed over him and there went any thoughts—dim or otherwise.

Then there was nothing but a wild need neither one of them seemed to know how to satisfy. It was all tangled limbs and rolling bodies and muttered curses that didn't quite make sense. They joined together in a storm that overwhelmed him completely, when he'd always had his two feet under him—good weather or bad.

But she was something wholly unique. He wasn't sure he'd survive it—or that he wanted to. Pleasure was an avalanche he wanted to be buried in. She rolled with him, coming apart in his arms, and he could only think to find a way to drive her higher, and higher, until something bigger cracked. Exposed them both.

She panted his name, but it wasn't enough. She set her teeth to his shoulder, shuddering and moving against him. But that wasn't what he was after either, even as she cried out. Over and over again.

"Connor. *Please.*"

Apparently that was what he'd been waiting for. Something exploded. Maybe his entire being. He was wholly and completely overtaken by light and sensation and something that felt oddly comparable to joy.

They lay sprawled out on the bed, breathing heavily. Connor stared up at the ceiling and could only assume she was doing the same.

"Don't get a big head, but I think I see stars."

He huffed out a laugh. He doubted Sabrina would ever let anyone have a big head, but he didn't mind the compliment. "I'll let you know what I see when I'm not dead."

She laughed in turn and rolled onto her side to look

at him. He eyed her, not moving since he wasn't sure he *could* quite yet.

"That was fun. I figure it could keep being fun when we're given the chance. That being said, I want to make it clear that fun is all I'm after."

He couldn't quite *laugh*, though the statement was indeed laughable. There was an odd pressure in his chest, but he ignored it and worked to sound as dry as possible. "And here I thought you were going to propose."

Her eyes narrowed a little at that. "Just trying to be clear."

"Well, you're crystal." And he was glad he was utterly relaxed enough not to delve into the odd pressure and be annoyed. No, he'd hold on to satisfied and loose. He nudged her onto her back, her dark hair spilling out over the pillow.

"I've got to let Froggy out." He looked down at her, balanced on his elbow. He couldn't read that expression, what odd mix of emotions swam in her eyes, and she didn't say a word.

She was strength and a brash confidence. She *was* the storm, and she wasn't going to let anyone forget it. But there was a beating heart at the center of all that. One with a big old melting pot of hurts and issues even he could tell she hadn't worked through. Why that should appeal to him on any level was beyond him. But it did.

She stared up at him—no snippy rejoinders or snarky smirks. Just…looking. She probably saw too much, but he figured he saw too much in her too. There was *some-*

thing here, between them, and neither of them probably wanted it or were comfortable with it.

But neither looked away. He kissed her before he fully thought it through, and didn't rush through it. He lingered, and something in his chest flipped, filled up, much like it had when she'd stood on that rock talking about destiny of all things.

He did not, would not, believe in destiny. And that included whatever this was. He ended the kiss and got off the bed.

"Get some sleep, Sabrina." He pulled on his pants and stalked out of the room to let his dog out. And hopefully get his head on straight. But he was a little afraid being with Sabrina had irreparably changed him, and he'd never be on even ground again.

SABRINA WOKE UP SLOWLY, burrowing into the pillow that…didn't feel or smell familiar. She yawned, not quite ready to open her eyes. She always woke up knowing where she was, but she found today her head was a bit scrambled.

Oh, right. She allowed herself ten seconds of pure satisfied smile. The guy had *moves*, and he used them *effectively*. She sighed because there was no time for a repeat performance.

Then she pushed out of bed because the sense of loss she felt over that was a little too close to her heart for comfort.

It was utterly dark, and the bed was now empty. Likely he'd stayed up to keep watch. Which meant it was his turn to sleep and hers to watch. And check her email.

If Nathan had responded maybe she could figure out a good next step. They had to move forward. They had to…not dwell here. In what had happened between them.

Inexplicably she thought more of that gentle kiss before he'd left her than the actual sex. Sex had been reaction. Great. A revelation, if she was being honest in the inside of her own thoughts. But that kiss…

It had been…

Nope. She wasn't going to think about that. She was going to think about her mission. Chalk up last night to a good time, *fun* just like she'd told him, and forget everything else.

She pulled on her clothes, ran her fingers through her hair. She didn't know where her hair tie had gone and her bag was still out in the kitchen. So, she'd just go get one. Go check her email.

Easy. Casual. No big deal. So, they'd had sex? Two unencumbered people who were attracted to each other could do that sort of thing and not have it *mean* something. Just because she'd never actually been able to go through with any one-night-stand type things even though she routinely pretended she did didn't *mean* anything.

Connor didn't *mean* anything besides a hot guy at the right place in the right time. She rolled her eyes at herself. She doubted that many people would consider *this* the right time.

She stepped into the kitchen area certain she was in charge of what she felt. He stood at the front door. It was open, though the screen door was closed. He was looking out into the night. The faintest hint of dawn was on the horizon. She could tell by his relaxed demeanor he was watching or waiting on Froggy rather than primed for a threat.

His hair was mussed. His feet were in thick hiking socks. She could smell coffee. It was like…living with someone. She didn't know why it was different than the other times in her life she'd shared quarters with a guy, but it was somehow more domestic. Cozier. Homier.

Or maybe it just felt different. What would it be like to just…watch the sunrise? With someone?

She shook her head, a little violently, hoping weird thoughts like that might just fall right out. She'd never had a thought like that in her life. And certainly didn't *want* to. There was no way she was pulling a Reece Montgomery and giving up her life at North Star for some sort of domestic bliss.

She'd be bored within an *hour*. North Star was her everything. The kind of risks she took were *necessary*. To her very soul. She barely knew Connor. She only knew his last name because *Shay* had mentioned it.

Take it down a few notches, Sabrina.

"Coffee's on," Connor said, rough and rumbly enough to have a flash of what it had felt like to have him inside her. "I figure you'll see if Nate emailed you back. If he did, we'll hopefully have a next step to move forward with. If not, I'll grab a few hours' sleep."

He opened the screen door and whistled. Froggy came bounding in, tongue lolling out to the side.

It looked like… It felt like… Like home. Not one she'd ever had, but the kind people with real families talked about.

She was really, really losing it. Coffee. She needed coffee. Maybe a lobotomy while she was at it.

"You okay?" he asked, and she realized belatedly he was looking at her. *Studying* her as she stood here and had some sort of break with reality.

She forced one of her snarky grins, though she wasn't sure it landed. "Peachy."

He quirked a smile. "I'll pour. You check."

She nodded and headed for her computer sitting there on the table. She ignored the irregular beat of her heart. How her hands were unsteady enough to type her password in wrong at first. She ignored everything except getting to her email.

Once she had coffee, everything would be fine. He put a mug at her elbow. She didn't look at him, though she grumbled a thanks. The email program booted up and Sabrina took a sip of the coffee as she waited for it to load.

Caffeine would fix the jangling feeling inside her chest. It would balance her right out. So she took a deeper sip, scalding her tongue in the process.

She put the mug down and swore quietly. "Nothing. Guess you can grab that sleep."

He didn't say anything, but after a moment or two his hand passed over her hair. Gently, not like the lusty tangle of last night. Her heart pinched dangerously.

"You better put this into one of those braids or it's going to be a problem."

She shook back her hair, eyed him. "Well, you know that makes me want to *never* put it up, right?"

"Because you like the problem, or because you just couldn't ever do anything someone else suggested?"

She didn't like how easily he saw through her, big surprise. The thing that was a surprise was that no matter how she told herself she didn't like it, she felt a bit like leaning into it. All of it. "I guess it's both."

"I don't mind both."

She had to say something mean. Something distancing. Something… Anything to stop this horrible feeling inside of her. Foreign. Weird. *Scary.*

Because it felt like hope.

But Froggy began to growl, low in her throat. All feeling had to be forgotten. The dog clearly sensed someone or something outside.

Connor muttered something to the dog and got the gun Sabrina had given him back when they'd been hiking. She already had hers in her hand. He signaled that he was going to check the back of the cabin and she should stay here in the front.

She nodded, surprised when the dog sat where she was and didn't growl anymore. Could have been an animal out there she was growling at, Sabrina supposed, but then again better safe than sorry.

She watched Connor melt into the shadows of the back of the cabin. Turned out, big, hot guy prowling with a gun was very much a turn-on. But she didn't have time to indulge it. Her phone was buzzing.

She looked at the screen. A text from Holden.

Don't shoot. Let me in.

Sabrina closed her eyes for one second. Just one, to try and find her equilibrium. What the hell was *Holden* doing here? "At ease, sailor," she called to Connor. "I know who's out there."

She was already jumbled up, thanks to Connor. But Holden showing up here... She had to get her head on straight somehow. She went to the front door as Connor reappeared. She opened it and Holden appeared out of the shadows like an apparition.

He stepped into the cabin as Sabrina held the door open for him. "What are you doing here?" she demanded.

"Had to save your ass, Killian." He grinned. "So you can come to my wedding." His eyes tracked over to Connor while Sabrina tried to make sense of *that*. "This our target?"

Sabrina looked back at Connor. The gun he'd been holding wasn't in his hand any longer. He had his arms crossed over his chest, Froggy standing next to him as if ready to attack. He looked nothing like a target and everything like the kind of guy who took targets out.

He said absolutely nothing, and Sabrina didn't know why she had to fight off the wave of a *blush*.

"Connor, this is Holden Parker. We work for the same group. Holden, this is Connor." She was about to say he was a former navy SEAL and could take care of himself. Like she wanted to defend him somehow. But that was stupid. *Everything* jangling around inside of her right now was extraordinarily stupid.

So, it was probably best just to keep her mouth shut.

Chapter Fourteen

Connor didn't like Holden Parker on sight. He knew it wasn't fair, and he found he didn't care. He watched Sabrina fetch the guy some coffee and a snack. They joked, took potshots at each other, and *clearly* enjoyed each other.

Connor found he kind of wanted to punch the guy.

He didn't, of course. He maintained his utter silence, no matter how many questioning glances Sabrina threw his way while she explained to Holden what they were doing.

This was their deal. Connor wasn't going to insert himself. He wasn't part of their group. He wasn't going to be *the target* either, but he'd handle that on his own. Their group could do whatever.

Connor was going to take care of himself. And Nate if it came to it. So, he stood in the kitchen, Froggy at his feet, listening to them and saying nothing.

Sabrina and Holden worked together like a well-oiled machine. Finished each other's thoughts, moving like partners in some kind of dance they'd been practicing for years.

No, Connor didn't like Holden. In fact, he wasn't ashamed to admit in the privacy of his own head that he downright hated the guy.

"I can't believe you're not asking about my wedding," Holden said after Sabrina had caught him up completely, down to the fact they were waiting on Nate's response.

Sabrina frowned at Holden. "I thought that was some kind of weird joke."

"Nope."

"You're...pulling a Reece?"

Connor didn't know who Reece was, but Sabrina was clearly shaken by the news of her coworker getting married.

"Not exactly," Holden said, the first sign of discomfort in a slight adjustment of how he sat. "Not exactly *not*. But regardless, we're finishing this first. I need to finish it for her as much as me and you. Her parents are spies."

"Her. This her got a name?"

"Willa. Willa Parker soon enough. Her parents are spies and they're the reason we got a name."

"I already had the name."

"Okay, sure." Connor didn't miss Holden's considering glance at him before it returned to Sabrina. "And you figured out the second target. But the mission I completed connects to this one. It's all part of a bigger picture. I want to finish it. For her."

"The bigger picture isn't my job." Sabrina stood abruptly, clearly irritated about something.

Connor could only assume it was the *her*, the wedding. That shouldn't matter to him. It *didn't* matter to him. He wasn't going to let it.

She paced, but then stopped herself and jabbed a finger over her shoulder to point at Connor. "My job is to save this guy's butt. And Nate's."

"I think we could save our own," Connor said, being careful to keep the acid out of his tone.

She whirled on him. "No, you couldn't. Because if I hadn't come along, you'd be deader than a doornail."

He hated that she was right. Maybe he would have sensed something was wrong in the moment. But her crashing his rescue had been the real thing that had saved his butt, and he couldn't be petty enough to argue with her about that.

"Gonna take Froggy out."

Sabrina looked at him like he'd grown a second head. "Aren't you going to add your two cents?"

"You two are doing just fine." He whistled for the dog and walked straight out the front door, Froggy at his heels.

He found a stick Froggy would get a kick out of chasing as the sun rose in the sky. It was going to be warmer than the past few days. Which of course put them at risk for another avalanche. Among other things.

He had to get rid of this edgy mood. He heaved the stick a few times, really putting some strength behind it. Froggy yipped and raced through the snow in perfect dog heaven, and it helped Connor even out.

At least until the door squeaked open and he looked back to see Holden there, studying him and his dog.

"She's in there taking a shower," he offered, coming up to stand next to Connor.

"Okay." Connor slid his hands into his pockets. He didn't know what to say to the guy. Didn't really feel like figuring it out.

"Just to be clear, it was never like that between me and Sabrina. Can't explain why exactly. It just wasn't. Isn't. So no need to be jealous."

"I'm not jealous." He wasn't so basic as all that. He just didn't like Holden. He had his reasons. He'd think of them. Eventually.

Holden slapped him on the back. A little too hard to be considered friendly. "Well, you're giving an *excellent* impression then." He sauntered back inside, and Connor felt no less like punching the guy in the nose.

Even if the fact Holden and Sabrina had *never* been something more than coworkers and friends to each other *did* ease something inside of him.

Last night had been a one-off. *Fun*, as she'd put it. That suited him fine. *Just* fine. What the hell other options were there? Zip, zero, zilch.

He turned to go back inside, beyond irritated with himself more than anything, but he heard the faint sound of…a helicopter.

He frowned and searched the sky. Surely he was hearing things. Or it wasn't really a helicopter. He'd sent Iona a text to stay far away. She wouldn't be so crazy as to…

Of *course* she would. She was a dog with a bone. Why was he surrounded by frustrating, irritating, *stubborn* women?

He swore. And stormed back inside to grab his radio and Froggy. Holden and Sabrina had their heads bowed over the computer. Sabrina's hair was wet and pulled back into a braid.

No matter what Holden had said, Connor didn't like it. Just plain old didn't like it. Because maybe Holden hadn't been interested in Sabrina, but that didn't mean the opposite wasn't true.

And it was absolutely neither here nor there, he reminded himself as he dug his radio out of his pack. "I hear a helicopter. I think it's Iona."

Sabrina swore herself and immediately hopped out of her chair. "You've got to get her out of here."

"I know it." He flipped his radio on. "I'm going to try to get her through this, but I've got to follow the helicopter."

"Con—"

He shook his head. "If she doesn't answer the radio, I've got to show her I'm okay and she's got to get out of here. She won't look at her phone up in the air. She's going to head for my cabin. See the fire remnants. If she doesn't hear me, she's going to have to see me, or this could get bad. Fast."

Sabrina was on his heels, but it wasn't necessary. "Stay here," he said, jerking his chin toward the table. "Keep working on this angle."

"Like hell I will."

He wanted to argue with her, but there was no time. He didn't need help trying to get over to Iona with the radio. He jogged north. It'd be a harder hike, but the straightest shot to his cabin was this way.

"You don't know what's out there," Sabrina said, hurrying to keep up with him. "They burned down your cabin. They could be lying in wait and you're going off half-cocked."

He glanced back at her. "I thought half-cocked was the name of the game."

She huffed out an irritated breath. "I don't know what bug crawled up your butt."

"That's funny because I know exactly what bug crawled up yours."

She stopped, but he didn't. "What's that supposed to mean?" she called after him.

The sounds of the helicopter were getting closer. He looked up, not bothering to answer her. It didn't matter. Him being an absolute *idiot* about her did not matter. Iona mattered. He pointed at the sky. "There," he said, calculating how far away from the cabin she was. How far away from him right now. "That's too damn close to my cabin." He got on the radio again. Tried to reach her. But there was no response. Connor swore.

A gunshot rang out and the helicopter jerked, the engine making a terrible sound as it hovered there, but only for a few moments before it began speeding to the ground.

SABRINA DIDN'T THINK Connor realized he was yelling as he ran. Making himself a bigger target than they already were.

Still, she couldn't blame him. His friend was going down and if the situation was reversed, she'd be doing the same thing.

Holden caught up with her. She'd asked him to pack everything up, hide her computer, and get all the weapons he could while she went after Connor. It hadn't taken him long to accomplish it.

"What's going on?" he demanded.

"Helicopter pilot is a friend he works with on Search and Rescue. She's not military. Shouldn't be mixed up in this. But the bad guys can't be too far off, Holden. And if she crashes that tin can…" Sabrina thought of the calm woman with the dark hair, that Connor was her kid's *godfather*.

It was all wrong.

"If she's a good pilot, she'll make a decent enough landing," Holden said, running right next to her. Her pack on his back, no doubt loaded with most of her weapons. He had his own gun in his hand as they ran after Connor.

What neither of them said was the possibility that the gunshot hadn't just hit the helicopter, but had hit the pilot. That the helicopter could very well explode before landing.

There were a lot of bad scenarios that could happen regardless of how good a pilot Iona was.

Still, they ran after Connor. Sabrina had to force herself not to think about him or the mom of three. She focused on their surroundings. On places a sniper might be situated. Connor would focus on helping his friend. *She* would focus on making sure they didn't get killed in the process.

They heard the crash, a loud, echoing thud, the sound of metal crunching in on itself. All three of them seemed to find an extra gear inside of themselves to run just a little bit faster than they'd been running, but the dog still made it there first—just out of view—and let out a bark of alarm.

She could see the smoke, smell the acrid burn of it all. But when the wreckage came into view, it didn't appear to be on fire. Yet. And it wasn't completely crushed. There was a chance, if Iona hadn't been shot, that she could be pulled from the wreckage and be okay.

Please, God.

Still a good few yards ahead of them, Connor threw himself onto the helicopter and wrenched open the door not skidded into the ground.

Before they could reach him, he'd dragged Iona out. Her eyes were open and she seemed to be moving some of her own accord as Connor began to stride back the way they'd come, Iona in his arms.

"Chance it'll blow," he said through gritted teeth. "Get as far back to the cabin as we can."

"I'm okay," Iona said, though she sounded thready. Definitely in shock.

She was bleeding profusely from her head. But she was talking. White as death but alive. It was *some* relief. But until they really examined her, it was hard to feel relieved fully.

"She needs a doctor," Sabrina said, following behind Connor.

"I'll call Betty," Holden said simultaneously, his phone already out and at his ear.

They walked quickly, though not at the same clip.

Connor was clearly doing everything he could not to jostle Iona as Froggy stayed at his heels, with an unerring and surprising ability to keep out of the way of quickly moving feet.

"I'm really okay, you know, considering."

"Considering I pulled you out of—"

The explosion echoed through the white world around them. Bits of debris scattered about them, but nothing sizable as they were far enough away. Still, an echoing rumble came from farther off and Sabrina eyed the mountains warily.

"Great, another damn avalanche and our best pilot needs a hospital," Connor said through gritted teeth, clearly struggling to carry Iona without further injuring her. "Do you ever think?"

"Your concern is touching," Iona said dryly. But her eyes were drooping.

"She's losing it."

"I'm fine," Iona said. But she clearly, *clearly* wasn't.

Holden was talking to Betty on the phone in low tones as they reached the cabin. Sabrina rushed forward to open the door. Connor took her straight into the bedroom and Sabrina worked very hard not to think about what had occurred in said bedroom last night.

"I'm putting Betty on video." Holden held out the phone so Betty could have a decent view. Sabrina opened all the curtains she could, trying to suffuse the room with more light.

"Someone pull her hair away from the worst of the wound. Carefully," Betty instructed through the phone.

Sabrina watched as Iona tried to do it herself, but her hands fell limply at her sides after a moment. Connor obliged, carefully rearranging Iona's hair.

"I didn't lose consciousness," Iona said, but even Sabrina could tell her coloring was getting worse.

"Consciousness is good, but it could be fleeting." Betty instructed Holden where to hold the phone, Connor what to do. After a few moments of considering silence, Betty sighed.

"That head wound is nasty, and you're losing a lot of blood. You've got to get her to a hospital. They'll be able to see if there's a skull fracture. Dangerous swelling. All that. She needs tests I can't do remotely, and she might need a transfusion. You've got to get her to a hospital. How far's the nearest one?"

"A lot closer if I had a helicopter," Connor muttered.

"You'd need someone to pilot it," Iona pointed out.

Her eyes were drooping again, and Sabrina noticed Connor was holding her upright more than he had been. But she was still talking. Cognizant of her surroundings. It had to be a good sign. It had to mean she'd be all right.

"Closest hospital would be a good thirty-minute drive. But we don't have a vehicle," Connor said. His icy sheen of control was beginning to crack, but Sabrina watched him work hard to keep it in place.

"I do," Holden said. "Hid it a ways down the road."

"You'll want to drive her as quickly as possible. Keep her awake if possible, but if she loses consciousness it's not the end of the world. The most important thing would be getting her to a hospital that has available blood in less than an hour."

"I'll take it and get her to the hosp—"

"No, Connor, you're the target," Sabrina interrupted as Holden ended the call with Betty. "You can't take her. They could follow you. Connect you to Iona, and then what? She's a target, that's what. Holden will do it."

Holden frowned. "I came here to help you on this mission."

"This helps me on this mission. Betty said it herself. She needs a hospital. You know Connor and I can't take her. We're already too mixed up in this. But if you take her, they can't connect it."

"They can when I come back."

"Don't come back. Go to this future wife of yours. Go get married and live your life, Holden." And she found... Even as weird as it was, as reticent as she was for change, she meant it. The way he'd talked about Willa... Holden should have that.

"Do I have a say in it?" Iona asked.

"No," the three of them snapped at her.

Sabrina put her hand on Holden's arm. This was imperative. To everything. "Holden. Please."

He inhaled and didn't look pleased about it, but he eventually nodded. "All right. What's the name of the hospital?"

"Wilson West," Connor said, clearly not liking the direction this was going. "I don't think—"

"I'll put it in my GPS and get her there. You contact her family. Once they arrive, I'll take off. I'll..." He shook his head as if he couldn't believe he was going to say it. "I won't come back. But you're using the backup crew. Gabe and Mallory especially. They were on my mission. They understand some of it, and they're good. You use them, Sabrina. Give me your word."

It was Sabrina's turn to suck a breath in and agree to something even though she didn't want to. "All right."

"Don't do anything crazy." He grabbed her shoulder and gave it a squeeze. "Promise me, Sabrina."

"I promise." Which wasn't hard. Taking a chance wasn't always reckless.

Holden nodded. "I'll bring the car up. You know they're going to be looking for that chopper they shot down."

"And hopefully the wreckage and the avalanche will keep them busy enough to get you out of here with Iona. We'll handle whoever follows us here," Connor said. He was all military stoicism, but Sabrina knew. Whether she saw something in his expression or she just...*felt* it, she knew he was holding on by a thread.

Holden eyed Connor, and then Sabrina. "Good luck," he muttered, then disappeared.

There was a tense silence Sabrina didn't know how to fill. Even Froggy seemed torn with indecision, standing between them uneasily. When Holden returned with the car, they got Iona loaded up as best they could. She was in and out of consciousness and Sabrina found herself saying a little prayer as they drove away—something she hadn't done much of since her mother had been alive.

"If anything happens to her I'm holding you and

your boyfriend personally responsible," Connor finally snapped out.

Sabrina didn't know what she was feeling. She should be mad. Snap back at him. Or even keep her head and coolly dismiss him. But her heart just *ached* and when he tried to storm past her, she simply couldn't... She couldn't let it go.

She wrapped her arms around him. "I know you're afraid, but he's going to get her to the hospital and she's going to be okay. I'm sure of it." She wasn't sure she'd ever tried to comfort anyone in her entire life. It was more uncomfortable than healing from a career-ending injury.

She nearly let him go, nearly bolted, but that rigid hold he had on himself loosened, slowly, glacially. He rested his cheek on the top of her head, his arms coming around her. His breath came out in a tortured sigh.

"Hell, Sabrina, Iona shouldn't be part of this."

"I know."

"Why are they shooting at random helicopters?"

"That I don't know." Which was hard to admit. A little less hard when he was leaning on her.

"They'll be coming for us now. They'll want a body. They'll see our foot trail and blood. They'll know."

Sabrina pulled back, though she kept her arms around him. She looked up at his handsome, stoic face. Only something in the blue of his eyes seemed to give away that he was torn up over this. Worried about his friend. Stuck in something that had never had anything to do with him or what he'd done. Because he was just...a good, decent guy. Who wasn't afraid to fight for the right thing. To protect because it was *right*.

She moved onto her toes, pressed a light reassuring kiss she'd have to find some regret over later. "Then let's be ready for them."

Chapter Fifteen

Luckily his time in the military had taught Connor how to compartmentalize. Because he had been away from it, though, and because Iona had become as close as family, it was harder to simply set his feelings of guilt, anger, blame and worry aside. And he knew her husband and kids would be worried sick.

Sabrina helped. He wasn't sure how exactly. A hug shouldn't have helped. He couldn't remember a time he'd needed soft comfort to get through something difficult.

But it helped.

It also helped when she stepped back, seemed to physically shake all the hard stuff away, and sharpened. Like the weapon she was.

"All right. Here's what we know. We've got one hit man who shot at us. What we don't know for sure, especially now that we know they're shooting at *anyone*, is if he knew it was *you*—his target, or just knew he was being followed."

"I'm not sure it matters *why* he shot at us."

"No, I'm not sure either. But it might. The more information we have, the more we don't just stop them from killing you, the more we get to the bottom of it. Because you're not safe until we get to the bottom."

"Cheering."

She smiled. Not that flashing grin. It was softer that had the tiniest dimple winking to life on her cheek. Something in his chest turned over with a flop. He really wished that annoying feeling would stop happening.

"Why did they shoot the helicopter? They didn't know Iona was looking for me, and even if they did somehow figure that out, wouldn't it make more sense to follow the helicopter? Think she knew where I was and follow it?"

"They're here, on your turf, I think, because it's isolated. They could burn down your cabin and like you said, no one might know for days. But if someone sees it, they have to leave. Without you."

Connor shook his head. Something felt off about that. "If they wanted to burn down my cabin, and knew where it was, they would have come to it right away. Not tried to get me on a search and rescue ploy. Easier to off me when I'm sleeping in my bed, wouldn't it be?"

"Yeah, easier. Maybe they had to double-check identity first. Maybe they couldn't find your cabin."

"I'd be easy enough to find and verify."

"Okay. So, it seems like the hit man was supposed to kill you. But they burn down your cabin without you in it. Do they think you have something? Something they need to destroy?"

"If they think that, they're wrong."

"This all connects to Nate. And they're after you. Burn down your cabin…keep people away at all costs."

Sabrina paced, and it clearly helped her think, process, but it made the headache at his temple pound with a vicious throb.

He rubbed his head, trying to work his way through everything that had happened in a short period of time. The hit man had missed. Then there'd been a team to burn down his cabin. Or had it been more simultaneous than that. Not totally, because of the avalanche, but by the time they'd seen the fire, it had been mostly finished. His cabin had been toast. They'd been there at least by the evening he and Sabrina had camped out.

"What if—"

But Connor knew where her brain had gone. His had gone to the same place. "Nate sent me something. Or they think he did. The hit man's on me, but you made things trickier. They still need that evidence destroyed, if it's evidence, even if I'm still alive and kicking."

"You don't get mail delivered to the cabin this isolated. So, what? A PO box?"

Connor shook his head. "I use the SAR office as my address. If it was important enough to burn something down over, would Nate really send it through the mail?"

"Who knows? It'd certainly make it *look* unimportant. So, I'd say we've got to get to the SAR office. Without the bad guys knowing that's where we're headed, and without anyone connecting anything."

"But I didn't have anything in that cabin. They torched the place and I didn't have anything."

"Maybe they assumed you did. Maybe Nate made them think you did? There's a lot of maybes."

Maybes. It wasn't all that different than his search

and rescue job. A lot of factors, a lot of possibilities. Instead of one target though, he didn't know *what* his target was. And that was just like the military.

"We've got to get it. Whatever it is. *If* it is." Sabrina raked a hand through her hair. "First step, use my phone to call headquarters and see if they have anything."

"*And* to warn them."

"Yeah, okay. But be careful and vague about it. My number is untraceable, but we don't know what kind of surveillance these guys might be doing at your SAR place. We don't know how long they've been tracking you."

"Not long enough, or I'd be dead. Or so you keep reminding me."

She smiled again, sharper this time, but it didn't last when she handed him her phone. "Really careful, Connor. Not a whiff that anything is wrong."

He tried to take the phone, but she held strong as she looked at him like a scolding teacher.

Why he *felt* admonished was beyond him. "They probably already know. Iona would have radioed when she was going down."

"You act like you don't know. You act as dumb as possible. You hear me?"

"Yeah, I got it." He yanked the phone and she finally let it go.

He dialed the number to headquarters, thought about who would be there this time of day. Probably Gene Branch. Older guy, retired firefighter, who did more coordinating than anything else. He'd know if Iona radioed. He'd know if Connor had a package. And he'd be easy enough to talk around.

"Hey, Gene. How's it going?" Connor asked casually when Gene answered.

"Con. Good. Good. Quiet, which is good with you out of commission. Iona said you were taking a few days off. Kinda sudden."

"Yeah, sorry about that." Since he didn't mention Iona's crash, Connor had to assume he didn't know yet. *That* didn't add up, but he didn't know how to bring it up without tipping him off. "Had some family stuff come up. Just wanted to call and check to make sure I don't have a bunch of mail piling up there?"

"Matter of fact, a package came yesterday. Iona thought it might be important so she took the heli out to drop it off your way. Figured you were stuck in because of the avalanche. She hasn't gotten to you yet? Should have."

Connor knew he had to lie, but his mind remained stubbornly blank. Iona had the package. Iona had…

"Con?"

"Gene? Gene? You there? I'm getting nothing but static." It was a crappy lie, but at least it was *something.* Connor hung up and handed Sabrina her phone.

"What is it? What's wrong? You went pale there."

"Iona had the package. In the helicopter. You know, the one that *exploded.*"

Sabrina swore. Not only was the package no longer hypothetical, but it was…gone. Real but useless to them. "We have got to get a hold of Nate. He's got to email us back."

"We don't have time for that, Sabrina. You know it as well as I do. We're going to have to call him and screw the consequences."

She was leaning toward agreeing. "Let me check the email one more time. Talk to…" God, she wanted to talk to Elsie about what they could do to protect themselves. Protect Nate. But this kept spiraling to some new place she couldn't quite get a handle on.

He was right. No time. "Okay, we'll call. But we play it my way." She had *no* idea how she was going to play it, but they didn't have time to plan it out. Connor had been right about those guys coming after the helicopter wreckage and then them. They needed some kind of direction and then they needed to get the hell out of here before the bad guys caught up.

She'd already put the number to the ranch Nate was supposed to be at in her phone. Just in case. Just as a precaution. And here they were, needing it.

She felt nervous. Not about calling or even speaking to Nate. But that she was making things worse. Making the wrong choice.

But she was officially out of choices. She hit Call and listened to the ring with her stomach pitching restlessly.

"Revival Ranch. Becca speaking," a perky voice answered.

"Hi. I'm trying to get a hold of an old friend of mine. I don't have his cell phone, but I know he's staying at your ranch."

"Well, I'll see if I can help you out there. Who are you looking for?"

"Nathan Averly."

"Oh, sure. I think Nate's around." There was the shuffle of papers, then the plaintive wail of a child somewhere. *"Mooooom."*

"Shh, you're fine, Dane," the woman hissed in a whisper. Then immediately used that pleasant voice again. "Just, hold on one second. Who should I say is calling?"

"Brina. He'll know who I am."

Another muffled whine from a child and the sharp whisper of a mother scolding her kid. Sabrina muttered a curse under her breath, then covered the receiver. "Let's pack up. Be ready to hit the road when this is over."

Connor nodded and Sabrina put the phone on speaker and on the table. They began to work as silently as possible to get all their gear together and back in the packs as they waited for the woman on the other end. There were muffled words, children shrieking, a few barks.

"Sorry about that," the woman said. "You still there?"

"Yeah, I'm—"

"Here you go then. Nate. Phone for you."

There was the sound of rustling and Sabrina and Connor moved for the table, both positioning themselves over the phone, staring at it as if Nate himself might actually appear before them.

"Hello?" The voice was low, raspy and suspicious. And so very much Nate Averly that Sabrina almost felt like her knees gave out. They were getting somewhere.

"Heya, Nathan. Your old pal Brina here." She wasn't sure the flippant tone she was going for really landed, but hey, she gave it a shot. "You didn't answer my email."

There was a long, fraught silence before he spoke again. "The office manager here showed it to me just a few hours ago. I hadn't quite figured out what to make of it."

"Yeah, well, when I didn't hear back figured I'd give you a call. Catch up, you know? Funny thing. I got an old friend of yours with me."

At Connor's horrified look, she waved him off. "From the navy. Said you called him Skidmark back in boot camp."

Connor glared at her, but clearly got the message. "Hey, Nate. Bob…here."

God he was bad at making up names. And lying, apparently, based on the name Bob No Last Name and the way he'd hurried off the phone with the SAR headquarters. Why was that adorable?

"Ah, Bob. Good old Skidmark," Nate said, sounding half amused, half baffled. But he played along. "Haven't seen you since boot camp. And you're there with Brina. That's some…coincidence."

"Oh, yeah. Small world and all that," Sabrina said. "Bob's in trucking, just like I am these days."

"Trucking," Nate echoed. "That's…interesting."

"Uh-huh." *Think, Sabrina, think.* "Listen, I figure you can't come to the thing and all. That's fine. But Dad left me something he wanted me to send you. I was getting all ready to mail it out and there was a bit of a mix-up."

"A package."

"Yeah, my fault," Connor inserted himself. "I meant to deliver it, but there was a bit of a problem and the package got destroyed. Sucks to have a package destroyed like that when you can't retrieve the contents."

Sabrina nodded at him. Maybe he *could* lie.

"Destroyed. Well, Skidmark, that sounds about like your luck."

"Or yours," Connor returned.

"Listen, I've got to go."

Sabrina couldn't let him get off this call until she really knew that he understood what she was trying to relay. Until she knew he'd try to get them the information they needed. "Nate—"

"No, I get it, Brina. Sorry about the destroyed package. Good to hear from you. Take…care of yourself. Both of you."

"If I needed to get in touch with you again—"

"I'll get in touch with you when I need to. Got chores." He ended the call before she could protest any more. She swore.

"Look, it's frustrating, but I don't think we have time for this," Connor said.

"Right." She rubbed at her chest. "Damn, I hate an unfinished puzzle."

"I think I'd hate having my head blown off more."

She rolled her eyes at him. "Well, I'm not going to let that happen to you, hotshot."

He huffed out a breath, not quite a laugh but close.

"We got in contact. I think… I think he recognized my voice. I think he got the package hint. Or at least he'll place it in this whole thing. I can hope. We can hope. But we've got bigger fish on our tail for the moment. Let's go."

"We can't just run."

"I wasn't planning on running. At least not away."

Sabrina eyed him. "You want to go to your cabin?"

"I want to see what we're dealing with."

"I've got a team coming. They'll canvas—"

"Until that team is *here*, Sabrina, let's do what needs to be done."

She rubbed at her chest again. Everything was all off. But he was right. They had to move. She'd prefer to lead him away, just because… Just because. But it would be pointless. He needed answers as much as she did.

She shouldered her pack and Connor attached Froggy's special vest leash thing. Sabrina moved for the door and looked back when he didn't follow. He stood there, looking right at her. Then he said the most… confusing thing he could have said.

"Thanks."

"For what?"

"Hell if I know, but I feel a little less like tearing after Iona and punching your guy's face in."

"He's not *my* guy. He's my friend. Like a brother."

"You sure about that?"

"Yeah, I'm pretty sure how I feel, jerkweed."

"Jerkweed. That's a new one." He stepped forward, but only to hover there in front of her like some kind of hulking mountain. "You seemed worked up about him getting married."

"Because I literally saw him a week ago and he had no plans to *ever* get married. What happens in a week to change a guy's mind? With some woman he's never met. It's weird."

Connor shrugged.

"If Iona had waltzed in here, with no warning, tells you she's divorcing her husband and leaving her family to join the circus, you'd wonder what the hell was wrong with her, right?"

"Yeah. Point taken."

She smirked at him. "Jealousy looks good on you, though."

"Not jealous."

"Then what would you call it?"

He only grunted, which made her laugh. Lightened her spirits some, but she turned to open the door. He stopped her by cupping her face, that big hand curling under her chin and holding her in place. She could have smacked it away. Could have done any number of things to get his hands off her.

She never seemed able to though. He touched her, looked at her, and she felt pinned in place.

"I don't want you taking any unnecessary chances on my account," he said, blue eyes blazing. "I need you to understand that. You're not my savior. I don't need one of those. We work together."

"You're the target."

"I was a navy SEAL, Sabrina. I can take care of myself. I don't need you to do it for me. I don't *want* you to do it for me. Any more than you'd want me to do it for you."

She didn't want to be hurt by that. A silly thing to be hurt by. Luckily, when she tried to turn her face away he held tight, which let anger fill in all those hurt spaces. But before she could unleash it, he kept talking.

"I couldn't *live* with it, if you took some chance *for* me. You get that?"

And *that* was different than not wanting her help, or thinking he didn't *need* her help. That was…

Well, things she supposed she didn't have the right or time to think about.

"We have to go, Connor," she said, her voice tight.

"Yeah, we do."

But he pressed his mouth to hers, for far longer than they had. When he released her, he brushed past her and out the door. "So, let's go."

Chapter Sixteen

They hiked. Again. It was a nicer day, the cold was just cold instead of bitter. But the melting snow made for harder hiking. Things were slick, muddy and amidst all that reminded Connor of what he'd found here. A peace in nature and the comforting cycles of it. Cold followed by warmth followed by cold. The simple struggle of man against nature. And the wide expanse of all that sky, framed by those craggy mountains that reached for it.

Now, all that peace was ripped up because some guy had taken a shot at him and blown up his cabin over some military thing he'd thought he'd left behind. And Nate had given him no answers, no clues, nothing. Connor couldn't even take confirmation away from it. He *thought* he'd heard understanding in Nate's voice, but maybe all he'd heard was someone trying to get off the phone with his ex.

A woman Connor had now slept with as well. Not exactly a comforting thought. But he found he couldn't care the way he thought he should. You didn't go after your friend's ex, but the thing with Sabrina was… Well, out of his hands.

He wouldn't go so far as to call it destiny. She'd have to be alone in that belief. But it was something bigger than thinking she was good-looking. Something deeper.

He could smell the acrid smoke from the helicopter crash even as they hiked away from it. Distance was key until they had an idea how many men they were up against.

Men. Burned-down cabins. Assassins. What *had* Nate gotten him into?

Sabrina hiked behind him, talking to her boss on the phone, coordinating this team of hers. Connor knew he should be grateful for the numbers, but he didn't know Sabrina's team. Couldn't trust random, faceless members of some *group*.

He was wound too tight. He knew it. The conversation with Nate hadn't helped, because all it had really done was make it seem like maybe Nate knew what was going on but couldn't tell them.

The conversation with Sabrina hadn't helped because when he said things like that to her that gave some hint to what insanity was going on inside of him, when he kissed her, he had to start analyzing *why*.

And there was no good answer. Not one that made any damn sense when it came to a woman he'd known for less time than the average shelf life of a banana.

"My boss is sending a team to Montana to help Nate," she announced when she hung up her phone. "My team is already here. But they're on the other side." Sabrina cracked a small tree branch off a tree and used the snow as a canvas. "This is your cabin," she said making a big X in the snow. "Where would you say we are in relation?"

He took the stick she handed him and made his best estimate.

"Okay, so I've got four on the ground here-ish." She made four Xs. "They're going to have to hike around. They should be able to get a read on how many men are guarding your cabin and what they're doing. Watching? Waiting? Tracking? We should sit tight, let my team meet us here."

He eyed her in surprise. "When have you ever sat tight?"

She grimaced. "Not often. Definitely not my strong suit. But it's the smartest course of action. And before you get all snarky about me following the smartest course of action, remember I'm holding a gun."

"This isn't how you'd normally handle a situation like this. You're handling it on the safe side because of me." He wasn't sure if it was his pride that poked at, or something else he couldn't identify. But he didn't like it.

She raised her dark eyes to his. "And if I am?"

"Don't," he bit out, doing everything to keep the rising tide of anger banked down. He didn't even understand why he was angry. She was making a smart, safe decision. They should both be smart and safe.

But his cabin was gone and someone had upended his life. Not just these "bad" guys. Not just the military, but at this point, his own damn friends.

"So, I should go risk both our necks, instead of just my own?" Sabrina demanded.

"Yeah, if that's what you'd do anyway."

"Did it occur to you that *I* might not be able to live with it if my disregard for my own life hurt yours in some way?"

That surprised him enough to sidestep the anger for a minute. "What do you mean disregard for your own life?"

She shrugged restlessly, pacing again. Always with the pacing. A ball of energy. All those sharp turns of her mind. A recklessness, and yet a core of determination to get the thing—whatever the thing was—done. And under all those rough edges a vulnerability, not just in what had happened to her, but in her need to give comfort. Even if she didn't want to admit that's what drove her, there *was* a need. Or she would have stamped out any softness toward anybody by now.

He understood it, even though they were so different, he seemed to understand her. Even when she baffled him, she made sense. She felt right. Like some missing puzzle piece. Too bad the past few days had torn the puzzle apart.

"I didn't really think my life mattered all that much for a while there," Sabrina grumbled, then whirled and pointed a finger at him. "And you know what? That wasn't so bad. Because I turned myself into a badass because of it. But I also built myself a family because of it, and I can't say I'm at all comfortable with that realization, but there it is. So, we'll wait, Con. We'll wait."

He didn't have the first clue as to what to say to that. Mostly because he understood. Deep in his bones. He'd been there. Maybe in a different way. He had to assume her disregard came from her rough upbringing, when his had come from an immature cockiness that time and maturity had cured.

Then he'd come here and, because he hadn't been able to lie to his own family, had built something of his own.

"Two peas in a pod, aren't we?" she said with a smirk.

Because it felt a little too much exactly like that, he scowled. "Something like that." He stood in the trail they'd forged, and looked around. Trees and rock, sky and cloud. And he was waiting for strangers to help him stop this threat against him.

There were questions he hadn't asked, because they'd been moving too much. Because he'd been too worried about Nate or Iona. Because he'd fallen into bed with this woman and inexplicably wanted to keep her around.

"Your group is sending some people to help Nate. Sending some people to help us. What's the endgame?" he asked, unclipping Froggy's leash so the dog could sniff around for a bit.

"Stop them. Figure out who they are and who they work for so that whatever this is, is over."

"Why?"

She wrinkled her nose. "What do you mean why?"

"What does it matter to your group? Why did they send you here? How do you all connect?"

"I was supposed to stop the hit man."

"But *why*, Sabrina?"

She heaved out a sigh. "I'm not in charge."

"Don't pretend like you don't know. Or like it might

not matter. We've been focused on what Nate can tell us. What about what *you* can tell us?"

She pressed her lips together. "It's not going to give you anything, but a couple months back, we—my group—was contacted to figure out a mystery for this small…government agency."

"Government. Mother of God, Sabrina—"

"Let me finish. I wasn't point on that mission, just backup." She looked down at her arm then shook her head. "But what we discovered was a black-market arms dealer supplying a bigger bad guy organization."

"Are you sure it wasn't the government?"

She rolled her eyes at him. "Which led Holden and I to *our* assignments. Before we stopped the arms dealer, they shipped off some high-powered weapons. We followed the weapons with the assignment to stop the hits. From what Shay told me, Holden's assignment didn't stop a hit, but found an intermediary. The intermediary has been able to give my group some information, but we're still mostly working in the dark."

"For a government agency."

"Yeah, one that didn't want you offed, Connor."

"I left that life for a reason, you know. Not just because they kicked me out for no good reason, but because the red tape, bureaucracy BS doesn't help *anyone*."

"You're alive, aren't you?"

He didn't know what to say to that, or what to do with the direct, *sympathetic* way she looked at him. So, he said nothing. Did nothing.

"What's interesting, to me, is that they sent a hit

man for you before they sent one to Nate," Sabrina continued. "That we know of. I'm thinking whatever blew up in that helicopter was pretty darn important. It's why you became the target above Nate."

"Great."

"It means we have to make it look like we have whatever it was. We have to pretend like we know more than we do until we can get more information safely from Nate."

"Fantastic."

"Aw, don't be grumpy." She reached up and ran her fingers over his cheek, mischievousness lighting up her dark eyes.

She was trying to poke him out of his dour mood, but he didn't want to be poked out of it. He wanted to *brood.*

Hard to hold onto when she was this close, when she was grinning up at him.

"I don't need your protection." Maybe that was the crux of it, much as he hated to admit it even to himself. He didn't like being at the mercy of other people. Didn't like feeling like the helpless victim. Maybe it wasn't even a *like* thing. He'd never been in this position before. He didn't know what to do with it.

Sabrina's mouth touching his jaw eased some of those uneven edges though. Even as she said obnoxious things. "But I *am* your protector, Con. Need one or not."

It was hard to argue with her when she'd wound her arms around him and was pressing her distracting mouth to his neck. But there was something important at stake here.

"I'll take a partner, Sabrina. How about that?"

Her eyes flickered, all that smooth confidence scattered for just a moment. "I can be a partner, but I'm warning you I've never been a good one. Too cocky, too nasty and way too intent on doing things my own way."

"Yeah, like I haven't figured *that* out." He shrugged, not quite able to stop himself from tucking a stray strand of hair behind her ear. A gentle move when this was really not the time or place for gentle. "Something I seem to like about that."

She rose to her toes to kiss him, but a man appeared out of the trees and Connor gripped her by the shoulders, about ready to toss her behind him like he was some kind of human shield.

But the guy didn't shoot and even as Sabrina made eye contact with the man, she didn't bother to unwind herself from Connor.

"God, not you too," the man said, sounding disgusted.

But Sabrina only grinned. "Hey there, Saunders."

IT WAS A good team. Gabriel Saunders was former military himself, but a marine. Holden had handled a lot of Gabriel's training, so Sabrina trusted Gabriel to know what was what. The other three were more part-time North Star, like a reserves situation, they came to help when there was a need.

But they hadn't dedicated their entire beings to North Star like Gabriel and she had. She trusted them to follow orders, but it was Gabriel whose mind she'd use.

She'd prefer to plan with Connor, and that was a surprising development. She was supposed to trust North Star above all else, and she *did*. She just also trusted Connor as much.

God, she wanted way too much when it came to him. She didn't know what to do with it. It reminded her of the navy SEALs. She'd wanted that with her whole being and look where that'd gotten her. And *that* was just a thing. People were even less controllable than freak injuries.

And boy, did she not have time to deal with any of *that*.

After Gabe gave a general update to her and Connor and the team now that they'd met here, Sabrina pulled him aside. She wanted his input without the input of the reserves or, if she was honest with herself, Connor. Just to make sure she wasn't letting her feelings interfere with her decision-making skills.

"We're evenly matched," Gabriel said in a low voice. "I think we could easily take them out, but if we still need answers, we need more than to just take them out."

"You said they have four men," Sabrina replied. "We've got six."

"No, we have four."

She glared at him.

"Sorry, you're the handler here. Your job is that guy, not taking down the men."

"Does that guy look like he needs handling?"

Connor watched them with an expression she couldn't read. It certainly wasn't a happy or hopeful expression. Resentment almost? But that would be dumb. He wasn't dumb.

"Look—"

"No, Saunders, you look. He's the target, sure, which means we keep an eye on him. But let's not pretend the former navy SEAL over there is some run-of-the-mill civilian who can't protect himself. He can act like part of the team as easily as these reserves you've brought along."

She'd thought she wanted Gabe's opinion, thought she'd doubted her own impartiality, but it turned out, when push came to shove, trust was the only thing that mattered to her. And she trusted Connor. She might prefer to keep him out of harm's way, but she knew he wouldn't stay there. Just as if she was in his position, she wouldn't.

Better to use him. Use them both. "Six against four. We plan that way." When he looked like he was about to argue, she flashed a grin at him. "I'm the boss, Gabe."

He gave her a doleful look, both at her shortening his name and at using her position against him. "Six against four is still tough odds if we're not taking them out. They're standing around that cabin waiting for *something*."

For Connor. And maybe her if they'd rendezvoused with the hit man and had figured out Connor was with her. Was the hit man one of the four men? Or was there a fifth man in hiding? There was no way to be sure. She didn't have a picture or enough of a description to give Gabriel or his team.

"We need more intel." That was all there was to it. Irritating and obnoxious to have to wait. But there were no other options. "We stand down until we get word from the Montana team."

Gabriel raised his eyebrows. "You, Sabrina Killian, are suggesting we *wait* until we have more information, rather than wade into the fray and knock some heads together?"

The disbelief poked at her confidence, because she knew she was far too wrapped up in Connor for anyone's good. But even as she tried to sort out feeling from fact, she only knew how to listen to her gut.

She glanced at Connor. Froggy stood next to him. He had his arms crossed and that disapproving look on his face. She wanted to be somewhere else. Where she could irritate that brood off him. Where it could just be them.

Never in her life had she wished to be somewhere else on a job. Never. She should let Gabriel take over. Trust *his* instincts over her addled ones. She even opened her mouth to do just that.

But she couldn't. She looked at Gabriel and she *couldn't*. Addled by feelings or not, her gut was her gut. She'd always trusted it. She couldn't stop now. "This is the right thing to do. I know it."

Chapter Seventeen

Connor knew Sabrina trusted her team, but he'd taken some time to observe each of them. To decide if he was going to trust them too.

It was the way they deferred to Sabrina that did it. She told them to wait, they waited. Even the head guy. Connor knew he didn't agree with Sabrina's plan, but he didn't argue. He didn't huff off and do his own thing.

He listened. He followed. Connor had to believe if they trusted and followed Sabrina, he should trust and follow them too.

When Sabrina took a phone call, walking a ways away from the group, Connor watched her. She paced. Then, still talking, she looked up at him and her eyes unerringly met his. She kept talking in low tones as she walked toward him.

And even knowing whatever she was going to tell him was bad news, even knowing they were sur-rounded by her team watching them very carefully, he *wanted* her. With a visceral pull he simply couldn't— or wouldn't—fight.

She stopped in front of him, and he didn't touch

her. He didn't say any of the things he wanted to say to her. But the way she looked at him, it was almost like she *felt* it.

And boy, he was losing it.

"Yeah," she said into her phone. "Got it. Here he is." She handed him her phone. "Your old pal Nate. Secure line. Feel free to tell him whatever you need to. Make sure he tells you what we need to know too."

He looked at her, a few beats too long. She didn't move. Didn't look away. When he finally took the phone, he held her gaze. "Hello."

"Care to explain how you got mixed up with my ex?"

Oh, you don't know the half of it. But the question, and the edgy drawl of it almost felt normal. Almost. "Care to explain why my friend's in the hospital and my cabin's obliterated? Oh, and why I got shot at?"

There was a pause. "I know you told me to let it go…"

"I told you to build your life. That's different. Sort of." He couldn't keep looking at Sabrina and have this conversation. And still he couldn't break the connection without some kind of acknowledgement. He hoped it didn't cost her any kind of tough points in front of her team, but he took her hand and squeezed it before turning away.

"Yeah, well…" Nate's voice went muffled. "You sure this is secure?" Then he sighed. "Okay, Brina's friend here says I can be assured I can tell you anything without anyone being able to trace, hear or whatever. I guess I have to trust her. I wanted to keep you as out of it as possible, Con. I tried. But this is bigger than me. Bigger than us. It's huge. We're talking military corruption on a scale…"

Connor winced. It sounded a little too much like what he'd been worried about. Nate being a little too… conspiracy theory. A little too obsessed. Paranoia. PTSD. There was a guilt that wound through Connor that he'd never fully been able to work through. He hadn't believed his friend.

Nate wasn't his responsibility. Nate had gone home, healed and worked on this ranch. He had family and friends there. Connor had trusted them to help him.

And all this time, Nate had just been right.

"I know I sound crazy," Nate said, frustration edging his tone. "I know it. It's why I can't go to anyone. But I also know what I've found. What I sent you was evidence Rear Admiral Daria was selling off weapons to the highest bidder. It's what my informant back in the Middle East was *this* close to telling me, or if not telling me, getting me to the place I'd see it myself. It explains everything."

Connor could only blink. Rear Admiral Daria. The guy had been no different than any other officer Connor had come into contact with. Serious. Hard. Maybe a little vindictive at times, but what officer wasn't? It wasn't a job for the fair or faint of heart, that Connor had learned. Weapons. Military weapons to…anyone.

"I know it sounds like I'm making it up, but I'm not. After they kicked me out, all trails led to him. So, I dug. And dug. I finally got what I needed to prove it. I sent it to you because I wanted to have it in a secure place before I went after them. I didn't want to involve you, but you were there. You were discharged. You were already involved. So, I sent you the evidence I had—"

"It's destroyed."

"Yeah, Brina told me." There was another pause, as if Nate was deciding what to tell him. "I might have some backup of most of what I sent you."

"Nate…"

"You don't believe me."

"I've been shot at and my cabin is blown up. I believe you." He just didn't *want* to believe Nate. Still, wanting to bury his head in the sand didn't mean he would. "I just don't know what the hell we're going to do about it. They want me dead. They're really going to want you dead."

"It's not the first time people have wanted us dead."

But it was the first time they were specific targets, not just a uniform.

"I'm sorry you got dragged into this."

Connor looked at the Tetons towering around him. Then he looked at Sabrina, clearly needling that Gabriel guy over something and enjoying the hell out of herself. Sorry? "I'm not." Even frustrated, tired and lost… Connor couldn't be sorry. "Have you seen any sign of people after you?"

"No. I think they want that evidence taken care of first. Before I sent it off to you I'd think…maybe. It felt like paranoia more than actual threat, though."

But if he took Nate's paranoia at face value, that meant *all* roads led to him because they thought he could prove Daria was the bad guy here. "You'd think they'd have a bigger…"

It hit him then. They had a bigger presence. Somewhere close, but not close enough for Sabrina's team to notice. Suddenly Connor knew that had to be true. These men didn't know the evidence had been damaged, and that meant they thought he had it. If they thought it was in the cabin and they'd destroyed it, they wouldn't still be here.

He was their biggest target. He was what they were after. What they were willing to kill for. Which meant Connor knew what had to be done.

"I know what I have to do. You sit tight. Watch your back. And let this…team of Sabrina's help you. They want to help."

"They sent me their computer geek."

"The person who could get us a secure line so I actually knew what was going on? How dare they," Connor said dryly.

"All I'm saying is you got the baddest badass, almost navy SEAL."

"Yeah, it's a real shame your ex-girlfriend couldn't come save your butt. Would have been a real nice reconciliation story." It was bitterness that coated his voice, and self-loathing that had him stalking away from the woman in question.

Nate let out a short bark of a laugh. "Brina and I would *never* reconcile. Whatever we had was all…kid stuff. Doesn't matter now."

But it did. Somehow, it had to. "Yeah, well, I slept with her."

"I… I do not know what to say to that."

Nor did Connor himself. Just that it had to be on the table. Just that… Everything had to be on the table. "Just felt like clearing the air."

"Oh, no. No. *No*. Don't you go play hero, Con. No need to clear the air. No getting crap off your chest. Because you're going to come out of this in one piece and tell me to my face you fell for my ex."

"I plan to." He did. But there were risks, and since he planned on Sabrina's safety falling just a hair ahead of his own, the clearing the air had been necessary. "Listen to the computer geek. I don't understand this group at all, but I know they're doing the right thing."

"You sure about that?"

Connor looked at Sabrina, talking to her team. He didn't know why or how, but… "Yeah, yeah I am."

SABRINA WATCHED CONNOR talk to Nate with an intensity that she figured the situation warranted. Probably.

When he ended the call, he walked back to her slowly. He said nothing as he handed her the phone.

"Well?"

"I know what Nate's trying to prove that could get us both killed. But more important, I know that the four guys you saw are just the tip of the iceberg," he said to Gabriel.

Gabriel stood, and Sabrina knew he was about to bluster about how his team hadn't missed anything. Because in his position she'd do the same. Still, she slapped a hand to his chest. "Wait," she said to Gabriel. "Explain," she ordered Connor.

His mouth thinned. Guy did not like an order. He'd have to suck it up for today.

And he did. Connor explained his phone call with Nate, what they were dealing with, and the fact that he was the main and perhaps only target for as long as they thought *he* had the evidence.

Sabrina absorbed the information. She appreciated Connor's delivery. It was straightforward and devoid of any emotion or…interpretation. He laid out the facts so they could all form their own opinions.

She knew he had his own, but for the time being he kept them to himself.

There was a few moments of silence as everyone took on Connor's information. Sabrina didn't get the sense he was leaving anything out, per se, but he was holding something back

"Maybe we're dealing with a small group. And *that's* why no one's after the other guy yet," Gabriel pointed out, echoing Sabrina's own feelings on the matter.

"Maybe. We've got a hired hit man, that we know for sure. Some kind of explosives expert, because that cabin was blown to *hell*. We've got a navy SEAL rear admiral implicated." Connor held up three fingers. "Maybe I'm wrong, but if I'm a dirty military higher-up, I'm not fooling around with a couple random guys. I'm sending out everyone I can to end the threat to my position, my reputation, hell, my life. Because you're not just looking at getting kicked out of the military, you're looking at getting tried for treason."

"You'd want your group small though. Too many

people know, too many possible slipups," Gabriel said. Which she would have told anyone was Gabe's biggest weakness. Once he had a theory, he didn't want to deviate from it.

Sabrina had the uncomfortable worry lodged in her gut though that if Holden left North Star as Reece had, she wouldn't have much of a say in who became the other field team lead. A worry for another time.

"You're selling military grade weapons to the highest bidder, you've got a direct pipeline to some of the worst humanity has to offer," Connor said. He was calm. Not rattled or frustrated he was arguing his point with someone. Just setting out the information. Weighing it.

"He's got a point," Sabrina said, trying to match Connor's calm so she and Gabriel didn't start a pissing match. "People who'd do anything for a price, and won't talk, because they've got their own skeletons. You wouldn't only take four of those to save your butt. You'd take as many as you could get."

"We only saw four," Gabriel insisted.

"Here," Connor returned, as bland as ever. "Watching my cabin. There's probably some watching SAR. There might even be some tracking our hike through the mountains. We've got four *here* to deal with, but that doesn't mean that's all we'll have to deal with. And this guy, this military guy, he's somewhere too."

"You don't think he's doing his own dirty work," Sabrina said.

"No, but if there was evidence you wanted to have your hands on, wouldn't you want to be close?"

She hated that he was right. The kind of guy who risked everything for some extra money, who used the military and his position in it to pad his pockets… Then was willing to kill over it?

He probably wasn't doing the dirty work, but he wasn't hiding either. Not when he knew everything was at stake.

"Which is why we need to set a little bit of a trap," Connor said, bright blue eyes straight on hers. Only on her.

She knew what it meant, and she had to fight, really fight, to keep her tone and gaze calm in return. "Let me guess. You're offering yourself up as bait."

"Let me guess," he said, matching her attempt at a bored tone. "You're going to argue with me about it."

She wanted to. Desperately. But that was knee-jerk, and she had to think it through. "The problem with that is they're just going to kill you. It's hard to be bait when they just want you dead."

"Not if they think I have the evidence stored somewhere."

"Risky, because they could take a gamble that Nate knows where it is."

"They could, but if it's important enough to kill over, would they?"

"They'd have to believe you," Gabe said, piping up for the first time in a while. "They'd have to believe it wasn't a trap. That you're actually scared or desperate or *something* enough to give yourself up."

"I'm not talking about giving myself up. I'm talking about getting myself caught."

Chapter Eighteen

Sabrina whirled away from him. It was her only outward sign of distress. She kept the rest locked down, and Connor could sense how hard that was for her.

He probably shouldn't have been soothed by that reaction.

When she turned back around, it was with clear, fierce eyes and a determination he knew he'd struggle to fight his way through.

"They know I'm with you," she said, as if she'd won a point.

"Sabrina, we don't know that for sure."

"We know there's a pretty high probability they know you're with a woman. That hit man shot at *us*. We can't risk that they know about me just for the sake of your ego."

He scowled at her. "It's not my ego. This is *my* problem."

"The way I see it? It's Nate's problem. He made it North Star's problem, and that made *you* my problem. So buckle up."

"Your group is called North Star?"

She blinked. Paled. "I…" No other words came out of her mouth. Just a kind of strangled noise before she grabbed him by the arm. Roughly.

"Stay here," she ordered her team as she dragged Connor away from them. Froggy whined and Sabrina rolled her eyes. "You can come, too," she muttered.

So, Froggy trotted after them as she pulled him away from her wide-eyed team and into a small grove of trees.

"As much as I'm keen, this probably isn't the time to have your way with me."

"Don't be cute now." She slapped his chest in one final shove. Froggy whined between them.

"He deserved it," Sabrina told the dog, immediately starting to pace as he stood there watching her work through…whatever was going on in that hard head of hers.

And maybe it was inexplicable but all this frustration, worry and anger calmed his own.

"Do you ever get tired of pacing?" he asked casually.

"I pace so I don't punch you in the face," she muttered and then if possible, paced *harder*.

"You slipped up and told me your secret group's name."

She stopped pacing, looked at him with nothing but fury and maybe some self-loathing on that beautiful face of hers. "Yeah, well, I trust you. So, bite me."

Maybe she hadn't said it softly, or with any *positive* emotion, but he understood enough to know what her trust meant. Or at least what it meant to him.

"Sabrina—" He reached out for her, but she sidestepped him.

"I can't..." She scrubbed her hands over her face. "Look. I need you to listen to me. Seriously listen. Put aside the ego and the macho nonsense and—"

"I would, but since I wasn't relying on any of those things..."

She scowled at him. "Okay. Whatever. Just... I can't let you be the bait in a trap when the chance of survival is something like fifty percent at best. We don't know enough, except how dangerous they are. I cannot let you waltz in there knowing they could know more about us than we know about them—which definitely leads to your death, by the way."

"Would you let yourself waltz into the middle of it? Alone?"

"I would have. Once." She looked at him and that fury melted into something...softer. He couldn't say he understood it, only that it made his chest ache. "It took me a long time to figure out..." She sucked in a breath and let it out. "The thing is you spend your childhood getting kicked around, you figure that's the way of the world. That kind of behavior is what you expect from people and it's what you give people. It took me a long time, a really, *really* long time to believe there could be another way. So, I won't lie to you and say I would never do such a thing, but in the here and now, Con, we need to depend on each other. We can't do this alone. It's a death wish."

"It's not a death wish. I get killed in this, Nate blames himself to the end of his days. I don't want that for my friend. I also have a feeling you'd blame yourself, and I don't want that for you either. This isn't a disregard for my own life. It's the only way we figure out what we're dealing with."

"Then you have to let me go with you," she said stubbornly enough he wished he could beat his head against the nearest tree.

Instead, he dug in. "If we're worried about each other, we're not focused."

"Is that what they taught you in the SEALs? Not to depend on anyone? I've been there, Connor. It doesn't work. I... It's taken me years to fully get that through my head. Hell, a few months ago I managed to break my arm because I wanted to handle things on my own, and I was ticked off at Holden for a few good more weeks after that for stepping in and stopping the situation from getting worse."

He shoved his hands in his pockets. "I'm not jealous or anything, but I sure am tired of hearing about how great Holden is."

Some of that heartbreaking *earnestness* lightened on her face, and he supposed his, yes, stupid jealousy was worth it if it made her smile.

She stepped forward, curling her hands around his arms as if she was going to shake him. But she only held on. "If you've got a team at your back, you've got to use it."

He jerked his chin toward the people they'd left behind. "They're your team."

"And I'm yours." She tightened her grip, looked right at him. "I don't know what the hell I'm going to do about it. But I am your team and I am sticking. You hear me?"

"Yeah, I hear you. Hard not to when you're yelling in my ear." And he heard something in her words that she wasn't saying. So, he figured he'd be the bigger person and say them first.

He cupped her face with his hands. "I care about you, Sabrina."

She jerked a little in his grasp, like he'd punched her rather than said something nice and meaningful.

"I guess I care about you too," she muttered. Then she pulled herself away, shoving at his arms. "So, we go together. Stop arguing and let's get this over with."

"Then what?"

She stopped and though he couldn't see her face he figured there was a little bit of fear sneaking over her features. He had to believe it.

"Let's live through this first."

Connor planned on it.

SABRINA HATED THAT she felt jittery as she outlined her plan with her team. They would each try to take down one of the lookouts. She and Connor would move in toward the cabin. The assumption being that as long as the North Star team could get the four lookouts around the cabin taken out, the other teams would be called in.

Maybe even the head honcho. They'd rearranged Connor's pack so he had some smaller bags inside he could pretend housed the evidence they were looking for.

The vests Gabe doled out made Sabrina feel marginally better about walking into an open field. Of course a good hit man would just take the headshot, but…

God, she couldn't think about that. She had to tuck it all away. Focus on the mission, just like she always did. As the North Star team had come to mean more and more to her, she'd had to fight side by side with what had become her family and worry about them. She was used to this clawing feeling of panic and setting it aside to do what had to be done.

She didn't know why being used to it meant she couldn't eradicate it completely.

Her phone buzzed and she pulled it out, read the text message from Holden, then showed the screen to Connor.

Has to be hospitalized a few days, but prognosis good. The husband here now. I'll stick around make sure no one connects her. Take care of yourself.

Connor's expression betrayed nothing, but because she'd been staring at the guy for a few days now she saw the slight relaxation in his shoulders. He was letting one worry go.

"Guess I'll have to thank the guy," Connor grumbled as Sabrina put her phone back in her pocket.

"Guess you will."

He grunted irritably, making her smile.

They situated the comm units in their ears. Another connection. Another safety. Every piece of North Star armor helped her set aside her worries and nerves and focus on what she had to do.

She stood in front of her team and Connor once they were all packed up and ready to head out.

"All right, team, no one takes any chances. You take down who you can take down. You stay with your partner. You get anyone to talk? Dandy. They're tight-lipped, we'll figure it out. Our end goal is to get as many of this group here in this area with us, then capture as many of them as we can until we have someone who can get us the main guy. We want to avoid casualties if we can, but remember *your* life and the team's life is most important."

She looked at her team, all grim-faced and determined. She trusted them to follow orders. To make the best choices for the team. She wasn't sure she trusted her partner to do the same, but she cared about him and would do what had to be done to protect him.

Whether he liked it or not.

"Connor and I will move into the clearing by the cabin remnants. A lot depends on who comes after us, so you keep those comm units in. You update all changes in position and all men you take down. We have to be flexible and ready to change gears at any moment. If we lose our communications, it's your job to keep tabs on us. Stay with your partners. Rely on each other. Let's go."

There was a murmur of assent, then everyone paired off and moved in different directions. *Here we go.*

"Nice speech," Connor said as they headed straight for the heart of things.

"I do what I can."

"You would have been a hell of a SEAL, Sabrina."

The remark didn't hurt as much as she'd thought it might. Because didn't she know? She *would* have been. But it hadn't worked out. Still it was some kind of comfort or healing or *something* to hear someone who'd been there say it.

"I'm sure as hell glad you're here to fight by my side instead."

She'd known for the past few years that things had probably turned out better this way than if she'd been a SEAL. North Star suited her better, and she had the feeling she'd done more specific good as a field operative than a SEAL.

And *still* some little piece of bitterness she'd held onto, deep inside, finally smoothed out into acceptance.

Destiny. Here it was. She looked at Connor out of her peripheral vision. He didn't have Froggy leashed, but the dog moved by his side as if they were one.

She listened to her comm unit with half an ear. Teams saying they had targets within sight. Still, she and Connor moved forward stealthily until the cabin ruins came into view.

She looked at Connor. His expression was grim, but he kept moving forward.

"Target one taken out. No shots fired."

"Good," Sabrina murmured into her mic. "Move onto the next."

The next three went down in quick succession, and a cold ball of dread settled in Sabrina's stomach. "Well, that was easy."

"Too easy," Connor said.

"Way, *way*, too easy."

"Do any of the men match the hit man's description?" Sabrina asked uneasily as she and Connor began to slowly, calmly move for cover.

She felt as though they were being watched, but that was the whole point. Someone finding them. Someone they could use to get to the head guy. Someone they could use to take the whole thing down.

Surely they wouldn't just be picked off. Not without the evidence. Of course if the people watching them assumed they had the evidence, they could just kill them and take it. But that was quite the risk.

At least…to kill Connor over.

Sabrina's heart stuttered uneasily in her chest. *She* was the expendable one. Had they been shooting at her in the beginning too?

"I've got one that matches your description," one of the part-timers said into the comm unit. "The gun and ammo we've been looking for. Should be our hit man."

It was a relief, and yet Sabrina didn't *feel* relief.

"I don't like being out in the open like this," Connor said into the horribly stifling silence around them. "They're going to take us out, not take us in."

"Yeah." Not *us*, so much as *her*, but if he didn't see that, she wasn't going to point it out to him. Especially when she could *feel* something really bad was about to happen. Sabrina spoke quietly into her mic. "We're going to pull back. Something is off. We'll rendezvous in that wooded area on the east side. Pick one guy to bring and we'll try to get some information out of—"

Something exploded into her. A searing bright pain

she couldn't make sense of. She stumbled back, fell, her legs unable to keep her upright.

The snow was cold. So cold. God, she was cold. She writhed in pain, trying to escape the burning, tearing inside of her.

There was a high bark, a harsh curse. Then Connor's face wavered in her vision.

"What the hell happened?" he demanded.

She didn't know. She hadn't heard anything. But she looked down at the same time Connor did. Blood. So much blood.

Silencer.

"Sabrina. Sweetheart."

"Oh, God, don't call me that. I'm not that." She tried to look away from the unbearable pain. The hot spill of her own blood. But all she saw was a gaping hole in the vest that was supposed to protect her and the seeping wetness of her own life slipping away.

Connor was ripping the vest off of her, dragging her out of the open area. They wouldn't know if they were still being shot at until the bullets landed. "Silencer," she rasped.

"I know it." He swore some more. Just a constant stream as he pushed some wadded-up fabric to her wound. She didn't know how he was doing it, then realized somehow he'd gotten the dog to help drag her by the shirt.

Connor pushed one hand to the lump of fabric on her wound. She cursed a blue streak to match his own as he used his other hand to fire back.

Sabrina wanted to tell him to run. She wanted to

tell him it was no use. She wanted a million things, but she felt her vision going gray. Everything just dissolving in front of her.

"Told you," she said, trying to fight the gathering darkness, the fade even as her teeth began to chatter. "It makes a joke out of…Kevlar," she managed to finish. But the pain was buzzing in her head and she couldn't see anymore. Everything was black. Everything was gone.

And then so was she.

Chapter Nineteen

Connor had never known such terror. But he bore down on it. There was no place for it here. Not when Sabrina's life was spilling out of her in front of his very eyes.

He concentrated more on putting pressure on the horrible bullet wound in Sabrina's side than the direction he was shooting at. He didn't have time to worry about the hit man. He just had to get Sabrina to safety as quickly as possible.

Good Lord. The bullet had torn through her vest. Just tore the protective gear to pieces. Like she'd said.

He babbled things into his comm unit. Who knew what. The rat bastard had used some kind of silencer. They'd made a grave, grave mistake thinking the hit man was one of the four men the North Star team had taken out. Made a grave mistake thinking Sabrina was invincible.

Blame wanted to bubble up, but how could he focus on blame when she was torn apart like this?

It took too long. Too damn long for the North Star team to appear as Connor, with Froggy's help, had pulled her behind a boulder.

"Good God." Gabriel started shouting into his comm unit. "We need immediate medical attention. Immediate. Sabrina's been shot. It's bad."

Bad didn't begin to cover it.

"There is a hit man out there with a gun and ammo that can shoot through Kevlar. She got a gut shot. You have to get her to medical attention. Now. There's no time to find these guys. Just get her some help."

One of the women in the team pushed forward. "Let me field dress it. Then we'll carry her out to somewhere we can get transportation. Helicopter?"

"They'll shoot it down," Connor said, wanting nothing more than to lie down next to her. Than to carry her out of here himself.

He saw the flash of something out of the corner of his eye, far off, and knew exactly what and who it was. "Hide. He's got a silencer. And that ammo cuts through anything. So you get somewhere you can hide. Get her somewhere. Get the hell out of the way." Connor grabbed Froggy's face, looked into the dog's dark eyes. "Stay with her."

Connor got to his feet, but Gabriel grabbed him by the arm before he could take off. "Where the hell do you think you're going?"

Connor jerked his arm away, and narrowly held back from decking Gabriel. "To kill the son of a bitch." Nothing and no one would stop him now. "Watch after my dog."

"You'll get killed yourself," Gabriel said after him.

"I wouldn't bet on it," Connor muttered, though he'd broken into a run so doubted Gabe had heard him.

There'd have to be a team of hit men with that ammo out there. Maybe there was. So bright and bold was his anger, his fear, Connor was sure he could take them all down. Piece by piece with his bare hands.

He shut off everything going on with North Star. Shoved away the feel of the woman he loved's blood on his hands. Loved. He'd used that stupid word *care* because he'd been a coward. He'd been too overwhelmed by something as stupid as a *feeling*.

And now he was going to pay the price. But if he had to pay, so would the man who had shot her.

Everything faded until there was only the cold grip of righteous anger.

The hit man wouldn't get away with shedding one drop of Sabrina's blood.

So Connor moved through the trees, around boulders, with only one goal in mind. Get to the hit man before he got another shot off. What he'd do once he incapacitated the man? Well…

It wasn't like being back in the military. This was no team mission. It wasn't the partnership Connor had agreed to back before Sabrina had been shot.

This was him. And vengeance.

He had the place where the hit man had been in his mind, and he worked toward it with a single-minded ferocity that left room for nothing else. Not worry. Not grief. Not pain. Not even the sound of his own footsteps.

He moved with a stealth he hadn't had since his days as a SEAL, but it all came back to him. Because he needed it.

As he closed in on the area he knew the hit man had to be in, or had to have run from, Connor made careful circles. He had a gun in his hand. He'd lost his pack somewhere along the way. If he'd had time, he would have lost the vest too.

It didn't matter except that he simply didn't have the time to shrug it off. Connor heard a sound. The faintest scrape of boot against rock. He stilled, listened, then crept forward with all the silence of a shadow.

When he skirted around another boulder, there was the man he'd rescued just a few days ago. He was laid out flat on a rock. Even if they'd had a sniper of their own, they wouldn't have been able to shoot him from anywhere except exactly where Connor was.

The man either didn't know Connor had left the group, or didn't think he'd come after him. He didn't look concerned at all. He had the rifle positioned to shoot, and he patiently watched through the sight.

Connor didn't know if he saw anyone. It didn't matter. He was a dead man.

Bigger fish to fry.

Alarming that his inner voice now sounded like Sabrina. Snarky and sharp and fully capable of sending this guy to hell, but choosing not to because there were bigger fish to fry.

Connor breathed through that rational thought. A deep, dark, desperately afraid part of him wanted to forget rational thoughts. Wanted to act only in violence. As long as he wasn't sure Sabrina would live, what did getting the bigger fish matter?

But it mattered. To Nate. To the people he didn't

know who had been hurt or killed or left behind because of what Rear Admiral Daria had done just because he *could*. Just for some extra money.

It took time to wrangle those messy emotions. To separate them. To focus. He moved the aim of his gun from the man's head to the hand that was wrapped around the high-powered rifle.

Then for his own satisfaction, he whistled. And shot only when the hit man's eyes met his.

THERE WERE VOICES. Jostles. The pain made her want to fade back into that black world where nothing hurt. Where there was nothing.

But there was something she needed to do. She had to figure out what it was. Where was Connor? Where was Froggy?

Where was *she*?

She blinked, trying to make her vision work. People were carrying her, but she couldn't quite feel all the parts of her body. And everything was swirly with gray around the edges. Unfocused and dull. "What's happening? Where's Connor?"

"Don't move, okay?" It was Gabriel's voice. Strained. Because he was carrying her over his shoulder while someone pressed something to where the pain in her centered. "Almost there."

"Almost where?" She didn't know if no one answered her because they couldn't or because they didn't hear her. She wasn't even certain she had managed to get sound to come out of her mouth.

But she was alive. The pain. The jostling. Trying to make sense of anything meant she was alive.

"Connor?"

But he didn't come into her vision. She didn't hear his voice. She saw Froggy's paws, trotting alongside Gabriel's long strides. Surely Connor was here if Froggy was.

"Close your eyes," a calm, female voice said.

"Betty?" How had North Star's doctor gotten here?

Betty didn't answer. She was busy shouting instructions as she did things to Sabrina's body that she couldn't feel.

"Come on, close your eyes. Do it for me, Sabrina. Now."

Sabrina was a little afraid she was going to never open them again if she closed them, but she always trusted Betty to patch her up.

God, she needed some patching up. She couldn't even move her arms. Couldn't get her brain to do more than circle. So, she closed her eyes, and fought not to give in to the dark.

"There's a girl." Betty's voice. "Gabriel, gently as you can, she goes on the stretcher. Keep those eyes closed, Sabrina."

Sabrina did as she was told and the world around her seemed to move. Her stomach pitched. Pain stretched out from so deep inside of her she almost thought of reaching for the black instead of fighting it away.

But she was alive. Alive. She kept her eyes closed and tried to focus on the voices. Betty's especially.

Though it was just coming to her in snatches. The word *hospital*. *Too late. So much blood.*

Too late.

Too late.

It seemed like everyone around her was chanting it. Only when the stretcher seemed to jerk then settle, and Betty shouted, "drive," did Sabrina realize the "too late" chants were her own.

"I'm going to die," Sabrina said flatly. *That* was her destiny. Finally got her head on straight, found a decent guy where she didn't screw everything up by kicking him to the curb, and she was doing to die.

"You're going to let this puny bullet wound take you out? That's not the Sabrina Killian I know," Betty said, but Sabrina knew that tone.

It was the tone she used when she was lying to someone about how big the needle was going to be.

"Gabe. Hold her still. I'm going to sedate her."

"No. No, you can't—wait. Gabe? Where is Connor?"

She tried to focus on him, but he said nothing and his face was just a blur.

Which meant Connor wasn't here. Oh, God. He'd gone off to… No. No, it couldn't be happening.

"Damn it, someone has to get to Connor. Someone has to—"

"We're taking care of it," Gabriel said.

"You're here. You're *here*. You're not taking care of…" The pain was so all-encompassing it was like a blinding bright white light and she couldn't get the rest of the words out.

"Hold her down," Betty ordered.

But Sabrina didn't feel it. Something fluid and warm moved through her, and she lost what little grasp she had on the here and now.

Chapter Twenty

The hit man did not take getting shot in the hand very well. Not only did he howl and thrash, but also the guy wasn't even smart enough to grab his rifle before it went flying off the cliff he'd spread himself out on.

Worked for Connor.

He stood over the man, who was holding his hand and keening in high-pitched waves as he held the bleeding, mangled hand. Connor didn't want to touch him, so he didn't. He pressed his boot to the man's neck.

The man shrieked, wiggled and tried to roll away, but since his hand had been shot and he was using the other one to hold it, he didn't use his hands or arms to push Connor's leg away.

"What? You never been shot before?"

That seemed to get through to the guy. Some of the thrashing stopped. Some calculation began to filter into his expression amidst the pain. Cold eyes looked up at him.

Connor pressed harder. Revenge kept working its way through him, making him forget the promises to himself. "Tell me where your boss is."

"You'll kill me whether I tell you or not. So go to hell," the man rasped. He started using his good hand to try and push Connor's leg away, but it was no use.

God, Connor wanted to kill him. He had to believe Sabrina's team had saved her, would save her, but she could be dead.

Dead.

He pressed harder against the hit man's windpipe as the man choked and gasped for air. Pulling at Connor's leg with his good arm, but ineffectually.

If Sabrina was dead, this man should suffer the same fate.

But this wasn't who Connor was. A life for a life wasn't his decision to make. No matter what happened, he wouldn't let that be the man he was. It would make him no better than this subhuman life form. "Actually, no matter what you tell me, you're going to rot in jail. One route is just going to be more painful than the other. You tell me, I tie you up and leave you here to be picked up by the authorities. You don't tell me, I keep pressing. Maybe I should press somewhere else."

Connor repositioned himself meaningfully, giving him the right angle to crush his boot in between the man's legs if he let go some of the pressure on his neck.

The man shrieked and bucked under the boot at his neck. "Don't. Jeez. You want to go one on one with the boss? Fine. You want to send me to jail? Fine. Daria's in an off-grid cabin on Albert's Peak. Good luck, you dumb SOB."

Connor knew the spot, thought he had a good idea where the cabin was. Miles away. It was a disappointment, but he could cover miles. He could cover the whole damn earth if he had to. He would end this. No matter what it took.

Connor kicked the guy onto his stomach, ready to tie him up, but the guy *had* to just keep yammering on.

"They'll get me out, you pissant nobody. This is futile. You're *nobody*. High and mighty nobody. I'll be out of jail in seconds. Then I'll come for you and—"

Connor laughed darkly. "You keep dreaming. You're a murderer. No one's getting you out of that."

"Murderer." He scoffed as much as a man being held down in the snow could scoff. "So are you. Military, right? You kill, but I do it for profit and I'm the bad guy? I don't think—"

Connor timed and executed the hit perfectly so that the guy lost consciousness from one nasty blow. Then he didn't have to hear the rest of his crap or tie him up. He searched the guy for weapons or ID or anything. Found a wallet with nothing but cash in it, and some ammo. Connor shoved both into his own pocket then shimmied down the cliff face and picked up the gun the hit man had lost. Wouldn't be easy to maneuver with, but he wasn't about to let it stay here for when the moron woke up.

Connor looked around, oriented himself to the area, then set out. The biggest problem wasn't terrain—he'd climb, ford, plow through anything in his way. The biggest problem wasn't miles, he'd cover every last inch without a break. Maybe he hadn't been a SEAL for a while, but he'd been trained for precisely this. He could, and would, hack it through sheer force of will.

The problem was he was one man, with two guns, an out-of-range comm unit, and absolutely no idea what awaited him at this off-grid cabin. Daria wouldn't be alone. He might even know Connor was coming if the hit man had some way of communication.

But there hadn't been any communication device on the hit man that Connor had found. Not even a cell. How were they communicating?

Connor hoped to God there was *no* communication. It could give him the element of surprise.

He would use whatever came his way. Face whatever came his way. No matter what.

But he had to focus on the facts. The cool, grounding weight of them. What had happened? *Sabrina* had been shot. A trained hit man with a major weapon had shot *Sabrina* while they'd been out in an open area, moving slowly. Easy pickings, if he'd wanted them both. If he'd wanted Connor.

The hit man had hit her, because they *wanted* him and didn't think she was worthwhile to them. But they needed him. Alive and ready to take in.

Connor could use that. He had to use that.

He wasn't sure how long he'd walked before he heard something, or maybe even felt something. Just suddenly he knew he was not moving through the mountains alone. He curled his finger around the trigger of his gun, the bigger one loose in his other hand. He kept moving. Ready. Waiting.

A footstep. Connor didn't whirl at the sound, he carefully turned his body, aiming the gun toward the sound, scanning the area and—

"Hey, wait up."

Connor spun at the voice, ready to shoot. But the voice hadn't come from the same place the footsteps had come from. But he thought he...recognized it. And when the figure appeared, Connor felt some mixture of irritation and relief.

Holden. "What are you—"

From the side he'd heard the footstep someone else moved into vision. Connor whirled on the unknown quantity.

The guy held up his hands as Holden spoke.

"Connor, this is Granger McMillan," Holden said. "He's with me. Well, us now. Granger, this is Connor. Former SEAL. Desperately in love with Sabrina."

"What are you doing here?" Connor growled, scowling back at Holden.

He bit his tongue to keep from demanding how Sabrina was. He didn't want to know if she was dead. Better to keep moving forward with the belief she was alive, and he was fighting for something. If she was dead...

"She's in surgery," Holden said, far too gently to have Connor snapping at him for ruining his delusions.

Connor swallowed. "Will she..." God, how was he supposed to ask? How was he supposed to deal with this weight? He wasn't. They should move. They had to...

"We don't know. But she made it to the hospital and she's in surgery." Holden nodded toward the way Connor had been going. "So, let's end this for her. God, she's going to *hate* that. She'll live just to be mad about it for the next century. The big strong men saving the day."

Connor knew this guy who'd been friends with Sabrina for far longer than Connor had known her was trying to bolster him. It might have shamed him if he had any emotions left.

"Don't get too cocky just yet." It was a woman's voice this time, as a built blonde stepped out of the trees.

The two men who'd joined Connor frowned at her, but they didn't point their weapons at her so Connor supposed it was another one of these North Star people. Not the ones he and Sabrina had worked with either. New ones. They were slightly older-looking with more aura of…authority, he supposed.

She smiled coolly at Holden and then Granger. "Can't let you boys have all the fun, can I? As you said, Sabrina would really hate that."

"Who's manning the group while you're here?" Granger demanded.

The woman narrowed her eyes at Granger. "Not your group. Not your problem. Now, what's the plan?"

Connor could question it, or he could take the help. There was only one choice that brought Daria down faster, and him back to Sabrina faster. "If I believe the hit man, the head guy—the rear admiral who started all this—is in a cabin over here."

"Do you believe the hit man?" Granger asked.

"I don't know, but if he's not here, something or someone is."

"Then let's go," the woman said.

SABRINA FELT LIKE she was swimming through gray mists. Sometimes they'd part and she'd see lights. Hear an incessant beep. Someone's voice. But it was hard to stay in those moments because the gray crept back in.

When she finally managed to open her eyes and keep them open, it was Betty's face swimming in her vision.

"Guess you saved the day," Sabrina said, but the sounds that actually came out of her mouth didn't sound anything like the words she was trying to articulate. She frowned, tried to shift in the bed, but Betty's hand softly yet firmly touched her shoulder.

"There you are," Betty said, smiling kindly. "Stay still now."

Sabrina liked Betty. Much as she didn't like being hurt or sick, Betty had always been a soothing, calming presence. Holden always got bent out of shape about having to sit for the good doctor, but Sabrina didn't mind.

She stilled under Betty's hand, tried to hold on to the fact she had her eyes open, understood who she was with and what was happening, even if she was struggling to speak.

"I had to sedate you in the field so they could operate right away once we got to the hospital. Bullet went straight through, but it nicked some organs on the way, which isn't the best. They stitched you up. You're pumped full of drugs so you might feel woozy, sick, confused. You won't be able to move quite the way you're used to, but that's all right. It'll all wear off."

"I'm going to be okay?" This time her mouth seemed

to work, though her voice was weak and scratchy. Slow and slurred to her own ears.

"You're not quite out of the woods. Infection is always a concern, among other things. But you're strong and a fighter, so my money's on you."

"What happened? I mean, got shot, I know. But after? Where's Connor? Did we get the guys?"

Betty's smile stayed in place, but something flickered in her eyes that had Sabrina's blood running cold. "No need for you to worry about that. Your focus is healing and—"

"Betty, you have to tell me what's going on."

Betty sighed. "Well, it was worth a try. They're still out in the field. Shay sent Connor some backup."

"Who? Gabriel? The part-timers are fine enough, but—"

"Not the part-timers. Not Gabriel. Sabrina, you have to stay calm. Really, really calm. Okay? If you can't, I'll have to get the nurse to sedate you."

"Tell me what backup she sent," Sabrina said through gritted teeth, happy her voice was coming out stronger. She wanted to grab Betty's hand. Demand and squeeze and rage, but she couldn't get her body to work in quite that way yet.

"Holden went," Betty said, eyeing the machines hooked up to Sabrina.

"I told him not to get involved! I thought he was quitting! Shay sent him alone?" Everything hurt. Her brain was fuzzy. But Sabrina knew this was all wrong. And felt twin pangs of relief that two of the best men she knew were working together, and horror that two of the people she cared about most in the world were out in harm's way.

"You can't get worked up, Sabrina. You just had major surgery. And Holden's not alone in helping Connor."

"Who?"

"Well… Shay called Granger in for a favor on Holden's case. Then she figured you almost dying was reason enough to call him in again."

"Granger? But he quit. He refused to come back. He…" Exhaustion washed over her, but there was relief in it. "Holden *and* Granger?" She felt like crying. Everything hurt. She wanted that oblivion again, but tears filled her eyes. Holden and Granger had put themselves in danger to help Connor. To help *her*.

Three men she would have trusted with her own life. Quite the feat for someone who never thought she'd trust anyone just a few years ago.

"And Shay," Betty added.

That did it. That really did it. A tear leaked over her cheek, but just one. She fought the rest back. "Who's running the group then? Didn't anyone tell her when you're the boss you're not supposed to go back to field operative?"

"Sabrina, honey? Right now, we're a family, not a group. And the people who love you and are in a position to are out there making sure the guy who hurt you doesn't hurt anyone else. Also, Holden said you were in love with this Connor guy."

"Love?" Sabrina made a scoffing noise that made her body hurt, and her eyes sting even more. But one tear was all they got. Just the one. "Who falls in love in a few days?"

"Apparently, you. And Holden. I can't wait until you meet this woman he's going to marry. She's… You're just going to have to meet her. And visit her farm."

"Farm?"

"Yeah. A farm."

That didn't make any sense, but that somehow made it better. That it was nonsensical. Love sure felt nonsensical, and not just because she'd been shot.

But none of this was okay until they were all back. "When will I know they're okay?" Not if. Never if. Only when.

Betty took her hand. "You worry about resting up. You're not out of the woods yet. Sewing up organs is not easy on a body."

"Betty…"

"It'll take time, honey. You just rest up so when they get back, you can kick their asses for taking care of this without you."

Sabrina sighed. She couldn't relax, but she let herself stop trying to *will* her way into the situation she couldn't be part of. "You always know the right things to say." She thought about everything that had happened. "What about the dog?"

"We've got her. She's being taken care of."

Okay. Okay, she could deal with this. She could figure this out. Holden, Granger and Shay were out there helping Connor. Froggy was taken care of.

Now she had to figure out what she could do. "I need to talk to Elsie."

"You need to rest."

"Bet, I can't rest until they're okay. So, I'm going to need you to get me Elsie on the phone. And everything North Star has on this Daria guy. And… Look, if I can't be in the field, you've got to give me this."

Betty's lips were pursed. "Fine, but I'm warning you, you won't have the energy for it."

They'd see about that.

Chapter Twenty-One

About a mile away from where Connor thought the cabin was, they met their first guard, dispatched easily enough. And, even better, a comm unit stolen to give them an idea of what the enemy was doing.

They stayed together in teams of two. Holden with him, Shay and Granger together. Though he hadn't seen them interact with Shay, except for Holden, Connor found trusting them was easy. They were part of Sabrina's team. Her family.

They were all here for her.

Dark was beginning to descend, but they were getting close. Connor could hear the guards occasionally talk to each other. It didn't give a clear picture of where they were all stationed, but evidently it was serious business.

The guards didn't seem to have a sense of what they were guarding. Only that they were waiting for something, and Daria was holding all the strings.

"They don't know anything," Holden said after they listened to two guards have a conversation about wondering how long this would last. He scanned the area, nodded toward a tiny pinprick of light. "You think that's it?"

Connor looked around. At the moon. At the mountains. "Should be." There was only darkness and moonlight and that tiny orange glow. There weren't any lights on the guards, which would make it difficult.

"Something is lit up in your pocket," Holden whispered to him. "Might want to take care of that before we get any closer."

Connor looked down at his leg where the cargo pocket held his phone. The display shone through the fabric. Connor scowled and jerked it out, ready to turn it off completely.

But he stopped at the unknown number on the screen. Could be some spam call, but with everything so…turned upside down, he wasn't sure he could just ignore… "Hello."

He heard Holden curse bitterly next to him, but that was immediately forgotten at the voice in his ear. "Connor…"

He thought his legs might give out, but they didn't. Words piled up, but none of the important ones would squeeze out of his throat. "How do you even have my number?"

"Magic."

He nearly crumbled right there. She sounded tired. Raspy and drained, but she still infused that sassy, irritable note to her voice and God, she was okay. Going to be okay.

"Now, you have to listen to me. He's got explosives."

Connor's mind was reeling. He couldn't quite follow. She was…alive. In his ear. Warning him about…

"Who's got explosives?" Connor held the phone out between him and Holden so they could both hear what she had to say.

"Daria. He's been stockpiling them. I think they're in that cabin. The guys we caught on our initial move didn't know anything about it, but Elsie's been unearthing evidence on Daria and the explosives can't be ignored. I think he's going to blow the whole thing up. He's going to end the whole thing, destroy all the evidence, including the witnesses. But he's waiting for you, because he thinks you've got the evidence on you, and maybe even thinks you know everything."

"What about Nate?" Connor demanded, even as Holden typed something into his phone.

"Elsie's working on that angle. You need to worry about you. Connor, you go anywhere near that cabin, he blows it up. I'm sure of it."

"I'm not backing off of this, if that's what you're getting at."

"Why not? I had to."

"Yeah, because you almost *died.*"

"I'm still here, aren't I?"

"Thank God."

There was a slight pause. "You have three of North Star's best field operatives with you. Work with them. Please."

Please. He'd only heard her say that once before. A memory he couldn't afford right now.

"They're your family," he murmured, understanding what she was asking. Not just to work together, but to keep them safe. To not risk them because he wanted to end this.

"Yeah, they are," she said, but surprised the hell out of him by taking it farther. "I love them, but I love you too. So don't get exploded, hotshot."

Love. "Did you just say—"

"Gotta go. End it. Safely. Bye."

Connor had mostly forgotten Holden was next to him, listening in. He might have felt discomfort over the love thing. Holden hearing it. Sabrina saying it. Love in general.

But there was no time for that. There was only ending this.

"Texted Granger and Shay to come back. If we're talking explosives, we need a new plan."

"You know anything about explosives?"

Holden grinned in the shining moonlight. "You happen to be looking at an expert."

"Okay, so, we'll put you on finding them. Disarming them. What about the other two?"

"The other two," Shay began mildly, coming into view on a quick run that was almost utterly silent, Granger behind her, "and you, will take out the guards. Daria probably has a gun or something, but there's no way he's some kind of fighter hiding in a cabin like this. He's the weak link. Once we get to him."

"Except the part where he can probably detonate whatever explosives Sabrina was telling about."

"Holden and I move to the cabin. Holden searches for the explosives and I take out any guards who try to stop him," Granger said, clearly used to being in charge. "Connor and Shay take out the guards around the perimeter. Once it's clear, I will enter the cabin—"

"Daria wants *me*. I'll be entering the cabin," Connor interrupted.

"Daria wants you so it's a risk to give him you," Holden argued. "Granger and I go. My bet is the explosives are inside. You let *me* go into the cabin and—"

"You're not immune to explosives any more than Sabrina was immune to that special ammo ripping a hole in her Kevlar and her *body*," Shay said, barely restrained fury in her tone. "Any of us die, she's going to feel that on her head. We're not letting that happen. Plus, we need Daria alive. He's supplying these stolen weapons to *somebody*, and we need to figure out who."

"I don't care who. I care about ending the man who wants to end me."

"Fair enough, Connor, but our missions overlap. Take out Daria, without loss of life." She gave Connor a meaningful look. "And then build on what we learn from here to move up the chain."

"I can stop the explosives. I should—"

"We don't know the explosives are in there. We don't know what Daria does if somebody he's not counting on bursts in there." She took a deep breath. "Connor is right. It should be him."

Holden and Granger both mounted arguments, but they stopped whispering them harshly into the quiet night when Shay held up a hand.

Connor took the pause as an opportunity to plead his case. Not because he needed permission, but because if they were all on the same page… Well, that's what Sabrina would want. "He wants me, yeah, but he also wants the evidence he thinks I have. I go in there, and tell him I have the evidence hidden, maybe we can draw him out. I have what amounts to a bulletproof vest. He needs me, or thinks he does."

"You took the chance at laying bait when you and Sabrina walked into that open field. Didn't work so well, did it?" Granger said gruffly.

Shay eyed Granger, an exchange Connor couldn't begin to understand. But it wasn't the point.

"No, it didn't. But it proves my point. The hit man shot her, not me. Here I am, totally unscathed, and he had ample time and opportunity. They don't want me dead. Not yet."

"That's the plan then. Granger, Holden and I fan out and take out all the guards we can. Connor, you head for the cabin. You walk in, try to draw him out. Ideally by that time Holden's got a handle on the explosives and can work on defusing."

Shay pointed to the light. "Granger, east, Holden, west. I'll head forward then circle around the back. Got it?"

Everyone agreed, so she sent them on their way. Holden and Granger first. Before Connor could run forward, she stopped him. "You die, Sabrina is going to kill me. So keep your head about you."

Connor thought of Sabrina saying she *loved* him. Then hanging up. "She's not rid of me that easily."

Shay's mouth curved. "All right, let's go."

She disappeared into the night, and Connor followed

at his own pace. He had two guns and his head about him, as Shay had said.

He didn't come into contact with any guards, which he figured meant North Star had taken care of them all. A good sign. Connor made it to the cabin. He took a second, only one, to take a deep breath and focus.

This was about apprehending Daria without getting everyone blown up. Without getting himself killed. With the guards taken out, carrying two weapons of his own, Connor figured he had a good shot to come out on top.

He crept up to the cabin. He gave a brief thought to trying to rendezvous with the other North Star operatives just to make sure, but taking out guards might call attention to people coming. Connor had to use surprise to his advantage, and not let Daria get off any explosives before he and North Star were out of here.

Though the windows glowed, it was around pulled curtains. So, Connor couldn't get a look inside. He would have to break in, guns at the ready. No other option.

He really hoped Daria didn't have one of these Kevlar piercing guns. But, no other options. This had to end. He didn't want to die and let that be on Sabrina's conscience, but he couldn't live with this falling through his fingers.

He took one breath, then kicked down the door in one quick slam. He ducked back out of the doorway, ignoring the flashback to the Middle East and missions there. He was in Wyoming. Cold to the bone, and about to take down his former superior.

No gunshots exploded. No guards came running. Connor led with the gun. He didn't have the tactical gear he would have had as a SEAL, but he still had the moves, the knowledge, the understanding.

Rear Admiral Daria stood in the middle of a rough cabin. There was no furniture, no explosives, no debris. There was only a man Connor had once saluted.

"Rear Admiral. I'd salute, but my hands are full."

The man who'd once calmly told him he was being dishonorably discharged and had to lie about an injury merely sneered. He held no weapons. Wore no vest. He had what appeared to be a phone in his hand, that was it.

But he didn't seem scared.

"I would have preferred my guards to bring you here in chains, but I suppose the ends negates the means," Daria said, all cool, practiced authority. "I want that evidence Nathan Averly sent you. Or you're dead."

"Seems like to blow me up, you'd have to blow yourself up too."

Daria shrugged. Calmly. So calmly Connor's gut turned to ice.

He held up the phone, and that was when Connor understood that would set off the explosives. Daria might not look armed, but oh… He was armed. Where were the explosives? There didn't appear to be any doors to other rooms, and mountain cabins—especially off-the-grid ones—didn't tend to have basements.

Still, Connor knew they were somewhere. Had to be. "Put it down, Daria."

Maybe the explosives weren't here. Maybe Daria was holding someone else's lives in his hands.

But there was such a...resigned set to his shoulders. To his mouth. He might be calm, he might be authoritative but...

"I don't care if I have to blow myself up in the process."

There was a deadness in Daria's eyes. A lack of hope. A lack of will. This was a man at the end of his rope. A man willing to die rather than face the consequences of his actions.

And that was the most dangerous thing Connor could have come face-to-face with. Because he wasn't going to win the bluff, which meant he had to hope to God Holden had figured out the explosives. Where they were. How to defuse them.

Connor swallowed. Sweat dripped down his back even though it was cold. "All right. You got me. I've got the evidence right here. Put down the detonator and I'll hand them over to you. You can take them. Escape. Kill me. You can do all that. We don't both have to die."

The man's smile told Connor everything he needed to know.

They were dead already if Holden hadn't been fast enough.

"See you in hell, Lindstrom." And Daria pressed the button.

Chapter Twenty-Two

Nothing happened.

Connor nearly sagged in relief. Even as Daria began to press the button harder and harder, just plain old relief swamped Connor.

"It can't be. It can't be. I'm not going in. I'm not…" He trailed off, looked up at Connor and the guns.

The calm, resigned man was gone. His eyes went wild and then he flew at Connor.

Connor didn't shoot him. He thought about it, but that was what Daria wanted. To be dead. To have nothing touch him. Connor simply moved out of the way, but Daria only pivoted, reaching for the guns.

"It doesn't matter now, Daria," Connor said, fighting the man back. He was surprisingly agile, though he couldn't beat Connor for strength. "The evidence we have on you isn't even here."

Daria tried to wrestle the smaller gun out of Connor's hand. Connor tossed the bigger one toward the door. He couldn't fight with no hands, so he needed one free. Daria lunged for it, but Connor tackled him to the ground before he could get it. Then he went ahead and tossed the other gun too.

Threatening to kill the guy wasn't going to end anything. He wasn't afraid of dying, and that made for a very dangerous man indeed. Connor didn't need guns. He only needed his strength.

A figure appeared in the door. Connor couldn't look more than peripherally as he wrestled with Daria to keep him away from the guns.

"Don't kill him. It's what he wants," Connor ground out.

"No problem," Shay's voice replied. She stepped in, unerringly reached down and grabbed Daria by the arm—Granger doing the same to the other arm—in an easily choreographed move. Connor panted and watched as they tied him up.

"You two are quite the team."

They looked at each other, another one of those charged exchanges Connor didn't understand.

"FBI should finally be getting up here in the next thirty," Shay said, once Daria was effectively bound and gagged. "They'll take him."

Connor got to his feet. Looked at Daria. His eyes were wild and he still fought his bonds, but it was no use. It felt anticlimactic almost. They'd found him. Stopped him. No explosions.

Now what?

Shay and Granger stepped out of the cabin to meet with Holden. They spoke in low tones, but as Connor stepped outside, he didn't listen. He looked up at the sky.

Now what? It was over, but it didn't feel over. Because he was stuck here, while Sabrina was...

Alive. She'd not just spoken to him, she'd warned him about the explosives. Somehow, even bedridden with a bullet hole in her, she'd saved the day.

Shay approached him as they heard the sound of an incoming helicopter. FBI coming to clean up the mess.

"We did our part." Shay clapped Connor on the shoulder. "Now they'll do theirs."

Connor let out a long breath. Stars winked. The night air was cold. And this was over.

Or almost over. He still had one loose thread to tie up. He looked at Shay. "You got some time to talk about something unrelated to this mission?"

"I'll drive you to the hospital. That should give us some time."

THE SOUND OF the door opening made Sabrina want to scream. She was so tired of being poked and prodded every five seconds. The beeps. The machines. She just wanted out.

She wanted to be in the field with everyone. She wanted to be side by side with Connor ending it. God, he had to end it. Not *die* in the process.

And she couldn't deal with any well-meaning nurses when she was this churned up. When she didn't have any answers to what was going on up on that mountain and probably wouldn't until morning.

"My blood pressure is fine and I don't want any drugs. Could you please leave me the hell alone and let me get some sleep?"

"Well, that's some way to greet the guy you dropped the L-word on in the middle of a deadly mission. I guess I could let you get some sleep, but—"

She whirled, nearly ripping out her IV and causing a lot of pain in the process. She moaned in agony and closed her eyes against the burning ache of it.

"Sorry, shouldn't have surprised the gunshot wound victim. Shh. Shh. Lie still." She felt the bed move as he came to sit next to her. His hand touched her face. "Sorry, sorry."

"You're here," she said, keeping her eyes squeezed shut. "You're okay. Gabriel said it would take hours. It would… You're alive. Everyone?" *Please God, don't let me be hallucinating.*

"Everyone's okay."

Then she just started *sobbing*. It was possibly the most embarrassing experience of her life, but she couldn't stop. The tears poured out, even as Connor carefully, so carefully, gathered her in his arms. She covered her face with her hands, but the sounds coming out of her didn't stop.

It was *humiliating*. But he held her. Tight. He was okay. Everyone was okay. It was going to be *okay*.

"Geez, Sabrina. You gotta stop that. You're going to kill me."

She sniffled, miserably embarrassed and yet so damn relieved she couldn't do anything but cling to him. "I mean, I almost died, feel like it's only fair."

He chuckled into her hair. And just sat there and let her hang all over him like a dope. "I don't want to hurt you."

"Just tell me what happened."

"Well, you know, Holden and I saved the day."

She pulled back enough to look up at him. So broad and sturdy and here. Blue eyes calm and *here*.

She wouldn't cry again, couldn't survive the embarrassment. But it was a hard-won fight to find her normal self in the midst of all this relief. "Except for the part where I warned you about the explosives and Shay made the three of you hardheaded men actually work together rather than race in as the sole savior."

He frowned. "How did you know that?"

"Woman's intuition. Now, tell me the rest."

Connor blew out a breath. He studied her face, as if looking for some sign she was really half a step away from death. But he spoke as he studied her. Held her carefully. "He would have blown us up, that's for sure. So, credit where credit is due. Shay had the best plan, Holden defused the explosives, the three of them took out all the guards and I…"

"Brought the bad guy in," she finished for him.

"He's not going to talk. They'll have to put him on some kind of suicide watch. He was ready to kill anyone in his path, including himself, to make this not stick to him. Don't know what it'd matter if you're dead, but I guess some people care more about their legacy than others. Nate's got the evidence to make sure it sticks, though. Daria bought and sold weapons on the side. There's more to it beyond him, and I don't think Nate's going to give up on this until he goes all the way up the chain, but the threat to the both of us, the specific threat of Daria, is over."

"Over," Sabrina repeated.

Connor swallowed. Hard. He leaned forward and pressed his forehead to hers. "I love you, Sabrina."

She blinked. She refused to cry any more tears, but that didn't mean they weren't there. She'd said it to him. Over the phone. But he'd had to know and now he…

She didn't know what the hell they were going to do about it, and she was too tired to figure it out, but it was enough now. She loved him. He loved her.

"Say it again," she murmured.

He chuckled, humored her and even kissed her gently. Too gently for her tastes, but as long as she was hooked up to half a dozen machines, she'd give him a pass.

"I'm in the hospital for a few more days. Out of North Star commission for a lot longer than that, so I guess we've got time to figure out how this love thing works."

He got an odd expression on his face, but he smiled. "Yeah, we've got time."

Epilogue

Sabrina was a little irritated Betty was the one driving her from the hospital in Wilson to North Star base farther northeast.

Surely, Connor could have made the trip. He visited her every other day, but only in the mornings. Like he had things to do.

Probably back SAR-ing. Living his life. *Not* worried about her at all. And good for him. What did *love* matter? They had two separate lives and that was that.

She wanted to pound something to dust, and worst of all, didn't have the strength for it. Betty even had to help her out of the car. She had to *lean* on someone to walk.

"You want to go say hi to everyone, or you want to rest first?" Betty asked as she unlocked all the security features and ushered Sabrina into North Star headquarters.

"I want to burn everything to the ground," Sabrina muttered.

"Aw, just like old times," Betty said, her eyes dancing with laughter. "But maybe a rest would do you some good."

Sabrina grumbled something. She was home and Connor was *somewhere*. Holden was *somewhere*. And no one apparently gave two flying pigs that she had been released from the hospital.

Or they're avoiding because they know you'll be in a foul mood. She scowled at her inner voice, knowing it was right.

Sabrina leaned on Betty as they walked deeper into the house, but frowned when she heard the low sounds of a female voice she didn't recognize, followed by Holden's voice shouting out orders.

Sabrina scowled. "What's he doing here?"

"Guess you'll have to go find out."

Sabrina scowled deeper, but pulled away from Betty. She took ginger steps toward the big room they did training exercises in when the weather was bad.

"Stop," Holden was yelling at two fighting figures. "You gotta let the military stuff go. Stop fighting fair."

A red-haired woman sat next to Holden, and glanced up when Sabrina walked in. She poked Holden's shoulder and he turned around to look.

He crossed his arms over his chest, looked Sabrina up and down. "Look who's decided to finally join us."

Sabrina couldn't look at who Holden had been instructing because she could only stare at the woman next to him. She was willowy with green eyes and freckles.

Holden pointed at her.

"This is my wife. Willa. You missed the impromptu wedding, by the way."

Willa smiled, beaming with a sweetness Sabrina normally wouldn't trust. "I've heard a lot about you."

"I wish I could say the same." She blinked. "Betty told me you have a farm."

"I do. And we'll be having a more traditional wedding for you to come to eventually." Willa and Holden had their arms around each other's waists. Casually. Like they fit, and Sabrina found she understood that. The way someone could just click into your life.

She wasn't sure she'd understand how to give up North Star and live on a farm or whatever. How to give up who she was but…

Then she had to pay attention to who had been fighting, because they walked around Holden and Willa, sweaty and panting and…

Connor.

He said nothing. He didn't smile. He just took the bag of medicine Betty had been carrying for her and slid his arm around Sabrina's shoulders. "I can handle it from here," he said cheerfully.

Cheerfully.

Then he was leading her out of the room, into the hallway. She hadn't said a word. Couldn't. Didn't know what on earth she could say.

She was dreaming. Hallucinating. Or he was. She looked up at him. "Are you drunk or something?"

But he simply maneuvered her through the house. The house he shouldn't have known how to maneuver her through. Certainly not to her room.

Which, she realized as he gently nudged her inside, was hardly *her* room anymore. Her twin bed had been replaced by something much bigger. The bedding was hideous. But there was a dog curled up at the end of it.

Froggy.

Her throat clogged, but no. No, she'd already cried all over him. That was a once-in-a-lifetime thing.

She turned—couldn't quite work up a whirl—and pointed her finger at him.

"Tell me what's—"

"Shay didn't think anyone else was ready to step in to take your spot while you're rehabilitating. So she offered me the job."

Sabrina found her knees couldn't hold her and she simply sank down. Luckily the bed was right there to catch her. "But…"

"Obviously with years' seniority, you get the lead position back when you're back to a hundred percent," Connor continued casually, even as Froggy wiggled her way to her side, laying her head on Sabrina's lap as if she'd gotten the message she couldn't be jostled just yet.

"Seniority. Job. I don't…" She pressed a hand to her temples. "Are you telling me *you're* part of North Star now?"

"Of course. Rumor is you guys used to have three leads anyway, so I figure as long as I earn my keep while you're hurt, I can just keep being a lead too when you're back."

She blinked. None of it made sense. Or if it did she didn't know how she felt about it making sense. She didn't know…anything. Except he was standing there, his dog in her lap, and he was *smiling*.

"Why are you grinning at me?" she demanded, stroking Froggy's ears.

"Because I know you well enough to understand that despite the look of horror on your face and your demands for information, you're actually going to be happy about this."

"Oh, am I? And why would that be?"

"Because you love me. And you love North Star. And this way, you get both."

She swallowed. "What do you get?" she asked, her voice a squeak, if that. No tears. *No* tears, but she couldn't control the way they fused in her throat like a lump. Still, better there than on her face.

"The opportunity to do good. Not just save people who made a mistake, but innocent people." He crouched in front of her, meeting her eye to eye. "But most of all, I get you. I'd do a hell of a lot to have you, Sabrina."

She sniffed. Shaky and tired and…soft. So damn soft. "Don't know why I'd ever fall in love with a cocky, grumpy, former navy SEAL."

"Yeah, I couldn't say. But here you are."

"Here we are." She leaned forward, wrapping her arms around his neck, pressing her forehead to his just like he'd done to her in the hospital. "Just so you know, I'm never crying like that ever again," she said, even as one more tear escaped. It'd be the last one.

He wiped it away. "Good, I'd rather have a gun to my head than watch you cry again."

"You're North Star now. That just might happen."

"We'll deal."

"Yeah, we will." Side by side. Doing what she loved, with the man she loved.

It was better than all the dreams she'd lost, all the dreams she'd barely let herself have before him. "You believe in destiny yet? Because if the coin flip had gone the other way, I'd have been in Nebraska with the farm girl and Holden would have been saving your butt."

He made a noncommittal sound, nudging her back so she could lie down on the bed. *Their* bed. She looked up at him, eyes already drooping. "Admit it. Destiny."

He dropped a kiss on her mouth then stood up, patting his leg so Froggy jumped off the bed.

"Maybe just this once, destiny had something to do with it."

She smiled, but she couldn't keep her eyes open. Too much for one day, and her bed was so much more comfortable than the hospital bed. A bed she'd share with him. She reached out and he gave her hand a squeeze.

"I love you, Sabrina."

But she'd already fallen asleep, dreaming about a future of love and kicking butt. Side by side.

* * * * *

**WE HOPE YOU ENJOYED
THIS BOOK FROM**

H HARLEQUIN

INTRIGUE

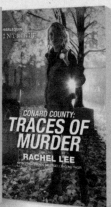

Seek thrills. Solve crimes. Justice served.

Dive into action-packed stories that will keep you
on the edge of your seat. Solve the crime
and deliver justice at all costs.

6 NEW BOOKS AVAILABLE EVERY MONTH!

#2043 PURSUED BY THE SHERIFF
Mercy Ridge Lawmen • by Delores Fossen
The bullet that rips through Sheriff Jace Castillo's body stalls his investigation. But being nursed back to health by the shooter's sister is his biggest complication yet. Linnea Martell has always been—and still is—off-limits. And the danger only intensifies when Linnea gets caught in the line of fire...

#2044 DISAPPEARANCE AT DAKOTA RIDGE
Eagle Mountain: Search for Suspects • by Cindi Myers
When Lauren Baker's sister-in-law and niece go missing, she immediately has a suspect in mind and heads to Eagle Mountain, where she turns to Deputy Shane Ellis for help. And when another woman seen with her family is found dead, their desperate pursuit for answers becomes even more urgent.

#2045 COWBOY IN THE CROSSHAIRS
A North Star Novel Series • by Nicole Helm
After attempting to expose corruption throughout the military, former navy SEAL Nate Averly becomes an assassin's next target. When he flees to his brother's Montana ranch, North Star agent Elsie Rogers must protect him and uncover the threat before more lives are lost. But they're up against a cunning adversary who's deadlier than they ever imagined...

#2046 DISAVOWED IN WYOMING
Fugitive Heroes: Topaz Unit • by Juno Rushdan
Fleeing from a CIA kill squad, former operative Dean Delgado finds himself back in Wyoming and befriending veterinarian Kate Sawyer—the woman he was once forced to leave behind. But when an emergency call brings Kate under fire, protecting her is the only mission that matters to Dean—even if it puts his own life at risk.

#2047 LITTLE GIRL GONE
A Procedural Crime Story • by Amanda Stevens
Special agent Thea Lamb returns to her hometown to search for a child whose disappearance echoes a twenty-eight-year-old cold case—her twin sister's abduction. Working with her former partner, Jake Stillwell, Thea must overcome the pain that has tormented her for years. For both Thea and Jake, the job always came first...until now.

#2048 CHASING THE VIOLET KILLER
by R. Barri Flowers
After witnessing a serial killer murder her relative live on video chat, Secret Service agent Naomi Lincoln is determined to solve the case. But investigating forces her to work with detective Dylan Hester—the boyfriend she left brokenhearted years ago. Capturing the Violet Killer will be the greatest challenge of their lives—especially once he sets his sights on Naomi.

"If need be, I could run my way out of these woods. You can't
run," Linnea added.

"No, but I can return fire if we get into trouble," Jace argued.
"And I stand a better chance of hitting a target than you do."

It was a good argument. Well, it would have been if he
hadn't had the gunshot wound. It wasn't on his shooting arm,
thank goodness, but he was weak, and any movement could
cause that wound to open up.

"You could bleed out before I get you out of these woods,"
Linnea reminded him. "Besides, I'm not sure you can shoot,
much less shoot straight. You can't even stand up without help."

As if to prove her wrong, he picked up his gun from the
nightstand and straightened his posture, pulling back his
shoulders.

And what little color he had drained from his face.

Cursing him and their situation, she dragged a chair closer
to the window and had him sit down.

"The main road isn't that far, only about a mile," she
continued. Linnea tried to tamp down her argumentative tone.
"I can get there on the ATV and call for help. Your deputies and

the EMTs can figure out the best way to get you to a hospital."

That was the part of her plan that worked. What she didn't feel comfortable about was leaving Jace alone while she got to the main road. Definitely not ideal, but they didn't have any other workable solutions.

Of course, this option wouldn't work until the lightning stopped. She could get through the wind and rain, but if she got struck by lightning or a tree falling from a strike, it could be fatal. First to her, and then to Jace, since he'd be stuck here in the cabin.

He looked up at her, his color a little better now, and his eyes were hard and intense. "I can't let you take a risk like that. Gideon could ambush you."

"That's true," she admitted. "But the alternative is for us to wait here. Maybe for days until you're strong enough to ride out with me. That might not be wise since I suspect you need antibiotics for your wound before an infection starts brewing."

His jaw tightened, and even though he'd had plenty trouble standing, Jace got up. This time he didn't stagger, but she did notice the white-knuckle grip he had on his gun. "We'll see how I feel once the storm has passed."

In other words, he would insist on going with her. Linnea sighed. Obviously, Jace had a mile-wide stubborn streak and was planning on dismissing her *one workable option*.

"If you're hungry, there's some canned soup in the cabinet," she said, shifting the subject.

Jace didn't respond to that. However, he did step in front of her as if to shield her. And he lifted his gun.

"Get down," Jace ordered. "Someone's out there."

Don't miss
Pursued by the Sheriff
by Delores Fossen, available January 2022 wherever
Harlequin Intrigue books and ebooks are sold.

Harlequin.com

HIEXP1221

SPECIAL EXCERPT FROM

(H)HARLEQUIN
ROMANTIC SUSPENSE

*Amina Kelly may be divorced, but she wouldn't
want her ex dead. When her ex is killed on duty,
Maxwell Layton comes back into her life—and the
passion between them is just as strong as ever. Now they
have to fix their past mistakes—while dodging someone
intent on making sure Amina doesn't get out alive...*

Read on for a sneak preview of
His to Defend,
the latest thrilling romance from Sharon C. Cooper!

"All of that's true and I hate this has happened to you,"
Maxwell said. "But you've forgotten one important fact.
You weren't harmed. At least not physically. Everything
in that house can be replaced."

"That might be true, but—"

"But you—" he kissed the side of her forehead
"—sweetheart, you're irreplaceable, and I'm glad you
weren't hurt. Now, *that*? That would've made the evening
a helluva lot worse. Because if that had happened, I
would be out for blood. We wouldn't be sitting here
together because I'd be out hunting that bastard. Instead,
we have others looking into the situation while you and I
are getting ready to try to salvage our date. So how about
we start by enjoying an excellent meal?"

After a long beat of silence, Amina sighed dramatically and leaned back to look up at him. A slow smile tugged the corners of her lips. "Well, when you put it that way, I guess I should pick a restaurant, huh?"

He grinned and handed her the menus. "Yes, and I'll take the bags upstairs, then change clothes. When I come back down, we can order." He stood and headed for the stairs again but stopped when she called him. "Yeah?"

"Thanks for coming to the house. It meant a lot to have you there with me even though I know it was the last place you wanted to be."

He studied her for a moment. "That might've been the case at first, but I want to be wherever you are, Amina. And I'll always be here, there or wherever for you. Remember that."

Don't miss
His to Defend *by Sharon C. Cooper,*
available January 2022 wherever
Harlequin Romantic Suspense
books and ebooks are sold.

Harlequin.com